The date! Pink p [when she lifted] **Mark, waiting for his reply.**

He'd been so focused on Sarah's condition that he'd forgotten he'd asked her out. Was her diagnosis the reason her previous love dumped her? Anger prickled Mark's insides at the thought. Who'd do that? In an instant his mind answered his question. *A Sanders man.*

Mark's eyes met Sarah's. He should stop this now. Tell her that he was out of line, asking her out. Explain about his dad. His heart pounded at the thought of hurting her feelings, but better now than later. He drew in a deep, steadying breath. He had to break the date.

ROSE ROSS ZEDIKER

lives in rural Elk Point, South Dakota, with her husband of twenty-eight years. Their grown son has started a family of his own. Rose works full-time for an investment firm and writes during the evening or weekends. Some of her pastimes include reading, sewing, embroidery, quilting, and spoiling her granddaughters.

Besides writing inspirational romance novels, Rose has many publishing credits in the Christian children's genre. She is a member of American Christian Fiction Writers. Visit Rose on the Web at www.roserosszediker.blogspot.com.

Books by Rose Ross Zediker

HEARTSONG PRESENTS

HP934—*Lily of the Field*

Job's
Tears

Rose Ross Zediker

Heartsong Presents

To Gert and Tome Stevens,
a real life MS heroine and her hero. Thanks for
your research help. Your friendship means the world to me.

A note from the Author:

*I love to hear from my readers! You may correspond with
me by writing:*

Rose Ross Zediker
Author Relations
P.O. Box 9048
Buffalo, NY 14240-9048

ISBN-13: 978-0-373-48613-7

JOB'S TEARS

This edition issued by special arrangement with Barbour Publishing, Inc., 1810 Barbour Drive, Uhrichsville, Ohio, U.S.A.

Chapter 1

"I don't know. Managing a business building may be too stressful with your recent..."

Sarah Buckley watched as Karla Ward, her best friend since grade school, swallowed hard. A lump of emotion no doubt. Even though the doctor had diagnosed Sarah with multiple sclerosis almost eighteen months ago, Karla still seemed to be taking it harder than Sarah.

Had Sarah known this was where their conversation would lead, she'd have chosen a corner table in the rustic coffeehouse chain versus this table in the open area where their discussion could be overheard.

Karla stared into space and tapped her paper cup on the high-glossed wooden table. Finally, her water-filled eyes close to brimming over, she looked at Sarah. "I just mean maybe now's not the best time to try a new career."

Sarah sighed, her good mood now dampened like her friend's eyes. Sarah had hoped for a little girl talk, wanting Karla's opinion on a man she'd recently met. Sarah thought he might be interested and wanted to bounce his actions off Karla. She shouldn't have agreed to meet Karla at the coffee shop before the evening quilting class that she'd looked forward to all day.

After two months, Sarah had a few doubts about her new career choice, but Karla's pessimism made her determined to maintain a positive outlook on all the changes in her life.

Maybe there was still time to turn the conversation around. "No time like the present." Sarah shook her fist in the air in a "go forth and conquer" fashion to show enthusiasm about the changes in her life and hoped it'd rub off on her friend.

Sarah earned a frown for her efforts.

"You are way too flippant about this. I think you need to go to counseling."

"Flippant about and counseling for what?" Sarah raised her eyebrows. "You can say it, Karla. Multiple sclerosis. I have MS. Dancing around the disease's name won't make it go away."

"I know that," Karla snapped. "I just don't know how you can be so accepting of your fate."

"What else can I do? We have to take the good with the bad." Sarah sipped her iced green tea. She wasn't ecstatic about her diagnosis, either, but since there was no cure for MS she had to find a way to live with it.

"Whatever." Karla's eye-roll answer didn't surprise Sarah. Her friend wasn't as grounded in faith as Sarah, who believed that if God brought you to it, He'd get you through it. At least she believed that most days.

"I have to earn a living." Sarah's MS forced her to quit the job she loved as a UPS delivery person. She couldn't tolerate going in and out of eastern South Dakota's hot, humid summer weather. It worsened her muscle spasms.

"That's just it, you don't. There are government programs."

"Stop." Sarah held up her palm. She'd had enough. "I'm not quite forty and only in the first stages of MS. Someday I may need assistance, but right now I just need a job that doesn't aggravate my symptoms."

Karla opened then closed her mouth. She pursed her lips and gave her head a shake, letting Sarah know she didn't share that opinion.

"I wish you were as excited about my new career as I am. The company I'm working for has excellent benefits. I'm in a temperature-controlled office, and I get to dress up. After wearing brown uniforms and comfortable shoes for twenty-two years, having wardrobe choices is a real treat." Sarah smiled before taking another sip of her tea.

"Congratulations," Karla said with a halfhearted shrug. She reached across the table and rested her hand on Sarah's arm. "You know I'm only concerned because I care about you. Right?"

"I know." Sarah placed her free hand over Karla's and squeezed.

Karla's concerned-filled eyes bored into Sarah. "I don't know that you're seeing the big picture with your disease. You need to take it easy."

Sarah did see the big picture. People in all stages of MS attended the support group she'd enrolled in. Many of the people in advanced stages of MS still led very active lives, just like Sarah intended on doing. She wasn't going to cower away in a room and watch life pass her by like Karla seemed to want her to do.

When Sarah didn't respond, Karla added, "I do have your best interest at heart."

I'm not so sure about that. Since her diagnosis, the one thing she thought wouldn't change was her friendship with Karla. Karla, usually supportive, saw only the negatives where Sarah's MS was concerned.

Sarah cleared her throat. "I need to get going. I have to pick up supplies before my class."

Karla released her grip. As she stood, she picked up her cup and said, "I never thought I'd see the day when you'd be sewing. At least you'll have something to fill your time when you find managing a building is too much for you with *MS*," enunciating the last two letters as if to prove she could say them. Karla then walked over to the waste can and dropped her empty coffee cup through the center opening.

Outside the building, Karla gave Sarah a loose hug. "I'll call you, and we can do this again."

Maybe, Sarah thought as she waved good-bye to her friend. Sarah needed optimism, but it was hard to maintain a positive outlook around Karla anymore. Idle minds were truly the devil's workshop. Sarah's own mind had hosted a few pity parties since her symptoms were diagnosed, which was the second reason she enrolled in the quilting class.

Please, Lord, change Karla's attitude concerning my illness and help me to adjust to the new challenges in my life. Sarah sent up a silent prayer as she walked to the other end of the strip mall that housed Granny Bea's quilt shop.

As the door buzzer announced her arrival, Sarah looked around. The quilt store appeared unmanned. Sarah's heart sank a little. She stepped forward and scanned the room's corners. Surely, *he* was here. Somewhere.

"Sarah, you're early." Mark Sanders, the store owner, came from the back of the building, his warm smile waking the butterflies in her stomach. "I was just getting the classroom set up for Caroline. Come on back and keep me company while I test machines."

The butterflies' fluttering wings lifted her heart and blew away all the negative energy from her visit with Karla. Reason number one for taking a quilting class—Mark. Sarah thought she preferred tall, lean men, but this shorter, stocky man sparked her interest. He'd been so welcoming on her first visit to the store. The way his eyes lit up when he looked at her made her feel special. Something she needed right now.

Now when the blues threatened her sanity, she found a reason to visit the store. Even after the briefest conversations with Mark, she left uplifted.

"I came early because I haven't purchased the fabric I need for my class project yet." Sarah held out the letter Caroline Baker, the class instructor, sent out with yardage requirements for either a table runner or a wall quilt. "I intend to use this coupon." Sarah pointed to the bottom portion of the letter that advertised 10 percent off supplies purchased at Granny Bea's.

"Don't worry about it." Mark waved his hand through the air. "You can get that after class. I read Caroline's synopsis, and she's going over quilting terms and sewing methods tonight. She gave me strict orders to have practice fabric available, so I don't think you'll need the project fabric until next week."

Mark led the way to the workroom in the back of the store.

"I'll be just a second." He turned to the right and went into a darkened room.

Sarah took a couple of steps past the threshold. The workroom stretched the length of the store. Three rows of folding tables roughly four feet long made up the classroom. A sewing machine sat at the ends of each table. *Mark must offer sewing classes in addition to quilting classes.*

"Have a seat." Mark rolled a plush office chair out of the darkened room and pushed it over by the first table. He held it steady until Sarah sat down.

"Thank you." Sarah smiled up at Mark as she took a seat.

"You're welcome." Mark continued to smile at Sarah for a few moments. His short light brown hair, combed straight back despite some receding on each side, accented her favorite feature—his eyes. The dark green polo shirt he wore today brought out the emerald highlights in his hazel eyes.

"You look like springtime tonight. Yellow is a good color for you." Crinkles formed by Mark's eyes as his smile widened.

Sarah's cheeks warmed. "Thank you." She'd bought the pastel crop pants set as her Easter outfit. Although it proved to be a little too summery for early April in Sioux Falls, South Dakota, she'd garnered many compliments at church, so she chose it to wear tonight because she wanted to look nice for Mark.

"You're welcome." Mark walked to the last plastic-topped table. He plugged a sewing machine into a power strip and pressed a button then repeated the action on the second machine.

Sarah lifted her left hand. Her fingers glided up and down the length of her dangly earrings. Shouldn't Mark be moving the sewing machines out of the way?

"How many people signed up for the quilting class?" Sarah smiled when Mark looked up from his work.

He moved to the second table in the row. "Five. One machine is for Caroline." Mark pressed a button and a machine lit up. When the second machine on that table didn't respond, Mark scowled and wiggled a power cord where it attached to the machine. He flicked a switch, seemed satisfied, and then walked to the front table.

"What type of sewing machine do you have?" Mark asked as he prepped the last two sewing machines.

"Um…" Sarah felt her eyes grow wide. She hadn't considered needing a sewing machine to make a quilt. She'd inquired about the classes to have a reason to talk to Mark. After a bout with the blues, she'd decided a hobby was a needed distraction. "I don't have one. I thought quilts were hand stitched."

Mark knitted his brows. "Not too many people quilt by hand these days. The first day you came into the store you purchased quite a bit of material, so I assumed you knew how to sew."

"My church was collecting sewing kits for a mission project." He remembered her purchase from three months ago? Of course he did. He picked up on her interest in the Job's Tears quilt block. What did he tell her that day? *"A good shopkeeper knows his customers"*— yet he made her feel like more than a customer. Was that his intention or her hope? She wished she could have discussed this with Karla, instead of the ongoing saga of her MS.

Satisfied that all the machines were on and in working order, Mark slipped his stocky frame onto the corner of the table closest to her and swung his legs. "I see. Do you know how to sew?"

Sarah dipped her head. She'd signed up for the class to give her a reason to be in the store. She'd been so focused on the feeling that bubbled inside her whenever she was around Mark that she hadn't considered needing or knowing how to use a sewing machine.

"No." She lifted her eyes like a child asking forgiveness. "Do I need to know how to sew before I can quilt?"

Mark laughed. "I think it would help, but Caroline used to teach home economics back in the day, so it shouldn't be a problem. If Caroline gives you quilting homework or you want to practice, feel free to come into the shop and use one of these."

"How sweet of you!" Relief that she could stay enrolled in the class infused Sarah's response, revealing a little more enthusiasm than she'd intended.

A deep crimson colored Mark's light complexion, but his eyes sparkled as he grinned.

"I me–meant to say that was nice of you." The warmth of Sarah's cheeks was an indicator that her face mirrored Mark's.

"I hope you take me up on the offer." Mark's complexion regained some of its normal color as he crossed his arms over his broad chest. "If you don't know how to sew, what prompted you to sign up for a quilting class?"

"Well…" Sarah stopped. Although she didn't agree with people who tried to hide their MS, she was tired of being pitied, so she phrased her response without making a reference to her disease. "I decided that I needed to fill some free time. I noticed all the beautiful quilts on display in your shop and thought quilting might be a good hobby. Then you offered evening classes, so I thought I'd give it a try."

Plus you make me feel special. Thank goodness that thought stayed in her head. Sarah fought the urge to fan the intense blush from her cheeks.

"I think you'll enjoy it. Job's Tears is a fairly easy quilt block, so you shouldn't get too frustrated with it."

"Can I hold you to that statement?" A storm cloud of doubts threatened Sarah's plan. Would she really be able to stay in the class if she knew nothing about sewing? Seeing Mark wasn't the only issue; without the class, how would she fill her free time? Guess it was a good thing that she waited until the last minute to purchase her supplies.

Sarah rested her hands on the rippled seersucker fabric of her crop pants. "Some of the quilts you have on display are so intricate. I can't imagine making one of those."

"Depending on the quilt size, block detail, and quilted stitch pattern, some quilters log hundreds of hours on a quilt."

"Wow." Sarah shook her head in disbelief. "I had no idea."

"It really is an art form."

Sarah nodded in agreement. A few silent moments passed. She tried to think of something else to say.

The deep breath Mark drew broke the quiet in the room. He rubbed his hands down his khaki pants.

Sarah noted Mark's body language. *Is he nervous, too?*

"I could show you how to work the sewing machine."

"You know how to sew?" Sarah's astonishment coaxed a chuckle from Mark.

"Just enough to demonstrate the sewing machines I sell." He slipped from the table and patted the seat of a folding chair in front of one of the machines. "But knowing how to work the machine might give you a step up in class."

"Really, you don't have to do this, I'm sure you have work to do." Although she hoped if he did that it could wait until class started.

"Nothing that can't wait until later." The legs of a folding chair squeaked across the tile floor as Mark pulled a second one over to the machine and sat down. He patted the seat of the empty chair.

Sarah's hands trembled and not from a tremor brought on by her MS. She arose from the office chair then hooked her fingers behind her back, hoping to conceal her nervousness as she walked over to sit beside Mark. Once seated, she clasped her clammy palms together and rested them in her lap.

Mark slid his chair closer to hers. "I'll show you the basics. Now these machines are older models and very simplistic." Mark reached in front of her and flipped a toggle switch. The light on the machine turned off. "Obviously, this is the On/Off switch." Mark flicked it, and the base of the machine glowed with light.

He leaned back just a little. "Back here is the lever to raise and lower the presser foot, which holds the fabric together while you sew." The metal piece that surrounded a needle moved up and down.

As Mark pointed to a broken-line symbol on the machine, Sarah tried to concentrate on what he was saying and demonstrating, but their close proximity goose-fleshed her skin. The hint of pine she inhaled with each of his movements fogged her mind, making it difficult to process his instructions.

"Now you try." Mark switched off the sewing machine's power and scooted back on his chair. He folded his arms over his chest. "Turn the machine on."

Aware of her rapid breathing, she inhaled deeply then reached up and flicked the On switch.

"Choose the stitch option."

Sarah stared at the panel filled with colorful stitch symbols. What had he said the standard stitch was? Straight? She thought it was the single broken line. She wrinkled her nose, closed one eye, and turned a knob until an arrow pointed at that symbol.

"Right. You're an excellent student. Now lift the presser foot."

The position of that piece on the sewing machine made it hard to see from the front. Sarah reached her left hand behind the machine and ran her fingers up and down the slender area of plastic. "All I feel is a screw of some type." She tried to peer through the opening of the machine.

"It's at the bottom of the arm." Mark reached up and put his hand over hers. His palm cupped her knuckles as he rested his long fingers over hers. The softness of his skin surprised her as he guided her fingers down the back of the sewing machine arm.

"Feel that?"

Nervous emotion clogged Sarah's throat. She nodded her response when Mark applied gentle pressure with his fingers as he escorted hers down a break in the plastic.

"That's the lever's track."

He continued the slow descent of their fingers to the bottom of the plastic cover. Sarah felt the blunt end of the lever tucked close to the bottom.

Sarah cleared her throat. "There it is." She stole a quick glance at Mark then swallowed hard to clear from her throat the giggle of happiness that his touch inspired. "I thought it was higher."

"I could tell." Mark removed his hand from hers. "Go ahead and lift up the presser foot."

Sarah raised the lever up with one finger. The presser foot rose to its upright position. She pulled her hands back to her lap and laced her fingers together, an attempt at composure. Her hands had trembled before, but now she was afraid of full-fledged shakes. She didn't want Mark to see how his touch affected her.

"Want to try sewing a seam?" Mark reached for some material that lay in the center of the table.

The door buzzer echoed through the store before Sarah had a chance to answer.

"Excuse me." Mark stood and walked from the room.

Fear wrestled with relief inside Sarah. If that was a customer, Mark wouldn't be back, and she'd lost her chance to spend more time alone with him tonight. Sarah had only felt attraction this immediate and strong one other time. She needed to get a grip on her racing pulse and come up with conversation topics. She couldn't let desire rule her heart and head again. She wanted to know Mark, not just be attracted to him.

Muffled laughter drifted through the workroom door. Sarah wished the room had a window in the wall, like the one in the short wall that separated the darkened office from the workroom. The laughter grew louder as Caroline Baker entered the room. She smiled over her shoulder at the tall man who followed her, laden with shopping bags. Caroline pointed, and he entered the office.

"Hi." Caroline smiled at Sarah.

Sarah stood up and walked toward Caroline. She extended her hand. "I don't know if you remember me—"

"Sarah Buckley." Caroline squeezed Sarah's extended hand. "Of course, I remember meeting you, here at the store earlier this year. You were wavering on whether you should enroll in my quilting class. I'm glad you decided to sign up, and I hope you'll enjoy it."

The tall, handsome gentleman came into the room and handed Caroline a canvas tote bag.

"I don't think you met my fiancé, Rodney Harris. Rodney, this is Sarah Buckley."

"Nice to meet you." Rodney grasped her hand, his rough, dry skin a contrast to Mark's soft touch.

"It's nice to meet you, too."

"Right this way." Mark stepped aside when he reached the door frame. A teenage girl and an older gentleman entered the room.

"I believe this is my cue to leave." Rodney pecked a kiss on Caroline's check. "See you at eight-thirty."

The door buzzer beckoned Mark back out to the main store.

"Have fun." Rodney waved to the quilters as he followed Mark through the door.

Sarah tried to focus on introductions and small talk, but every few seconds she glanced toward the door, hoping to catch another glimpse of Mark.

Mark led two more ladies into the room. "Your class is complete."

Sarah's steady pulse quickened when he glanced her way before he turned back to Caroline.

"Let me know if you need anything," he said as he closed the door of the workroom.

Sarah wished that she could have talked to Karla about this. She'd never had much luck with relationships, but she thought Mark seemed as interested in her as she was in him.

But she'd been wrong about that before.

Like a needle inserted through fabric, dread pierced Mark's heart as he walked to the cutting counter in the center of the store. He thought he had at least six weeks to get to know Sarah better. Since Sarah lacked sewing skills she might not stick out the quilting class.

Mark unrolled the last bit of fabric from a bolt. He measured the piece of material, cut it, and folded it into a fat-quarter square. If she quit the class would she still come to the store? Probably not since she didn't know how to sew. It made his day whenever her petite frame graced his quilt shop. She'd thought he was sweet to offer the use of one of the sewing machines. Would she think so if she knew he had an ulterior motive?

Mark looked up from his work when he heard the door.

"Here's your coffee." Rodney handed him a paper cup from the franchise down the block.

"Thank you for offering to bring me a cup. What do I owe you?" Mark reached into his front pocket for his money clip.

"My treat." Rodney sipped at a lime-colored cold drink.

"Is that green tea?" Mark grimaced and exaggerated a shiver.

Rodney chuckled at Mark's antics. "It is. It's good for you. Want to try a sip?" Rodney waved his cup close to Mark.

Mark smiled. "I'll pass and stick to the hard stuff. Thanks for taking the quilts to the back room."

"It's the least I could do. You looked pretty peaked when Caroline and I arrived. I thought you might be feverish. Your face was flushed. But then when I went into the workroom, I knew why." Rodney winked at Mark.

The heat worked its way back up Mark's neck and onto his cheeks as he remembered the silkiness of Sarah's ivory skin as he cupped his hand around her delicate fingers. He shrugged and sipped his coffee.

"Thanks for letting me hang around your store while Caroline teaches class."

"It's not like you're in the way." Mark looked around the store. "Business is always slow on Tuesday nights. That's why I scheduled a class tonight. I thought the activity around the store might bring in more traffic. Judging by the sales floor it doesn't look like that theory works."

"Maybe you should run a Tuesday night special. An extra discount after seven or a 'buy one yard of a fabric, get one yard for half price' deal. Or would that cut into your profit base?"

"The discount wouldn't. The fabric might, but I guess I could run it on certain fabrics or clearance fabric. I might just give that a try." Mark emptied another bolt and began to measure the fabric.

"Gonna ask her out?" Rodney shook his cup, bouncing the ice against the plastic.

Mark ran his sharp shears down the grain of the fabric, separating it into two pieces. "I plan to, but I don't know if she'll accept. She's a little out of my league."

Sarah was a classic beauty. Long dark lashes fluttered over coal-colored eyes. Her small pug nose with the slight upturn at the tip led down to plump lips. He even liked how her short black hair was cut to show off her dainty ears.

Mark laid the scissors down and folded the fabric pieces.

Rodney scowled at him. "What do you mean by that?"

Mark pointed his index fingers at his body and waved them up and down. "I'm not exactly Mr. GQ. What would a petite beauty like Sarah want with a middle-aged guy built like me? That's what I meant." Yet she did seem interested.

"You're solidly built inside and outside. That's an asset, buddy." Rodney gave a curt nod to punctuate his belief.

"Thanks." Mark knew Rodney meant well trying to build his confidence, but Mark was a Sanders. Sanders men were solid on the outside but not so much on the inside where it really counted.

"At least you know you'll see her five more times. You can build up to asking her out." Rodney peeked over the counter. "Got a trash can?"

Mark motioned for Rodney to hand him the cup and pitched it into the trash under the cutting counter.

"Maybe. I'd hoped to speak with Caroline before class, but everyone seemed to arrive at once. I found out tonight that Sarah doesn't know how to sew."

"And she enrolled in a quilting class?" Rodney frowned.

Dread poked at Mark's heart as if it were a pincushion.

"She thought all quilts were sewn by hand. I know Caroline won't kick Sarah out of class and will try to teach her to sew, but I'm afraid she might get frustrated and quit the class. Job's Tears isn't a hard quilt pattern, but for a beginner it might be."

Rodney rubbed the back of his neck with his hand then smiled. "I guess if she does, you'll have to offer basic sewing classes. I know a really good teacher."

"Does Caroline pay you a commission to be her agent?" Mark finished folding the last of the fabric before he grinned at Rodney.

Rodney laughed at Mark's teasing. "Guess my pride in Caroline overflows."

"Sure does, but that's a good thing." Mark wrapped a paper strip with the Granny Bea's logo printed on it around a square of fabric. He pulled the protective paper from the adhesive on the strip and secured the ends together.

"That's why I'm encouraging you to ask Sarah out."

Mark stuck a price sticker on the fat quarter and picked up another square to package. He didn't really need encouragement. He planned to ask Sarah out. Would she accept was the question.

"I'm not looking for a serious relationship." History proved Sanders men weren't good at commitment.

"Are you sure? Having the love of a good woman

makes life complete." Rodney pulled a weekly ad-filled paper from his pocket. "I'll just sit over there and leave you to your work."

Rodney and Caroline were the quintessential happy couple. Like all couples in love they wanted everyone else to be in love, but sometimes attraction was enough.

Sarah said she'd enrolled in the class to fill some free time. He'd seen her features darkened when she thought no one was looking as she browsed the store. Something troubled her. It didn't take much to put two and two together—a bad breakup.

He'd been the interim guy many times. It worked for him. Mark told the ladies up front he wasn't looking for anything serious. After he helped rebuild their self-esteem and he refused to get serious, they'd break it off with him. It was a win-win situation for everyone involved. The ladies regained their self-confidence, and he dated a beautiful woman for a few weeks before they went their separate ways. No strings. No hard feelings. No broken hearts.

He glanced over at Rodney studying the paper. A stand-up guy like Rodney wouldn't understand Mark's dating philosophy. Mark wasn't a love-them-and-leave-them type, but he was his father's son, so short, no-strings-attached relationships were in the best interests of both him and the ladies he dated. He'd never been wrong about that before.

Chapter 2

Sarah gathered all the handouts Caroline gave the class, tapped them to straighten them, and then laid them on the end of the table in a tidy pile. Hopefully this stalling tactic would ensure Sarah would be the last to leave the workroom. She needed to confess her inability to sew to Caroline. After a few polite good-byes and see-you-next-weeks among fellow class members, attendance finally dwindled down to just Caroline and Sarah.

"Did you enjoy the lesson?" Caroline picked up papers and the Job's Tears quilt block templates and tucked them into her tote bag.

"Very much." *When I could stop worrying about not being able to sew or see Mark again.* "I do need to talk to you, though." Sarah walked to the front of the room and stood beside Caroline.

Caroline stopped gathering her supplies and devoted her attention to Sarah.

Sarah bent her neck to look up at Caroline. She almost came to Caroline's shoulder. Sarah moved back a step to allow for a more comfortable conversation.

"Shall we sit?" Caroline slid a folding chair away from the table for her student then grabbed the office chair and rolled it closer to Sarah.

After they were seated, Sarah looked Caroline in the eyes. "I have a problem."

"What is it?" Caroline's blue eyes searched Sarah's face before returning to Sarah's gaze.

"I don't know how to sew."

Caroline's jaw dropped.

"I thought quilts were hand sewn, like in old movies that show quilting bees." Sarah hurried through her excuse, not giving Caroline a chance to respond. "Will my inability to machine sew mean I need to give up this class?" Sarah fingered the earring on her left ear.

Caroline pursed her lips together, not in an angry or annoyed way, but more like she was trying to stifle a giggle.

Embarrassment snapped out and wafted down over Sarah's heart like a blanket being thrown on top of a bed. How could she have been so naive about this? *Because, Sarah, you weren't really doing it for the right reason.*

Caroline gave into her grin. She reached over and squeezed one of Sarah's hands. "I guess I have an authentic quilter in my class. I don't run across many of those anymore."

Sarah knitted her brows together but smiled back at Caroline, some of her discomfort fading. "I don't know if I can be called authentic or a quilter, right now."

"In six weeks you'll be both. I promise you. Now, if

you're more comfortable sewing your quilt together by hand that's fine with me. Sewing quilts on the machine is so much faster that it never crossed my mind that someone might want to make a quilt the old-fashioned way. I may offer that option to everyone."

Caroline withdrew her hand and rose from the chair.

"Keep in mind, though, that sewing the blocks by hand takes longer, so you may fall behind during class and have to catch up on your own at home."

Sarah stood then pushed her chair under the table. "Mark did offer to let me practice sewing on one of these machines." A small thrill shivered through her as she remembered his touch during the demonstration of the sewing machine. "So I'm not sure which way I'll go with the project, but at least I know I can sew the quilt by hand, and I don't have to drop out of the class. See you next week."

Sarah practically bounced out of the workroom. Things seemed to going her way, and it showed by the spring in her step. Whether she sewed by hand or came in and tried to learn to machine sew, both would occupy her free time. *And I'll get to see Mark.* Sarah's thought widened her smile.

"What did you do that the teacher punished you by keeping you after class?" Mark stood by the cutting table in the center of the store.

Sarah chuckled at Mark's teasing and walked over to his work area. "Staying after was my choice. I wanted to make sure that I wouldn't be holding the class back with my lack of sewing abilities. Caroline assured me that I could be an authentic quilter and sew the blocks by hand if necessary. So, I'll need to get my fabric picked out."

"No time like the present." Mark held his arms out wide. "You can have your own private shopping spree."

"Don't you close in fifteen minutes?" Sarah asked as she noted the only person in the store was Rodney, who rose from a chair in the sewing machine display area and walked to the back of the store.

Mark glanced at the clock that hung above the full glass door. "Yes I do, but if you know what you want, you can pick it out, and I'll get it measured and ready for you to pick up another time."

"Well…" Sarah paused, weighing her options. She did have the fabric narrowed down to two different patterned pieces and the solids to coordinate, but she hadn't quite decided between the two. "I think I'd better wait until I have more time to decide. I'll stop by after work some night this week."

"I'll be here. Unless it's Thursday. I'm on a men's bowling league that night."

Was that a subtle hint to come in the store when he was working? "I'll probably stop in tomorrow night after work, then."

"Where do you work?" Mark slipped a pair of scissors under the cutting counter.

"I'm employed by Card Leasing. I manage an office building in the new development area close to the junctions of Interstate 229 and Louise Avenue." Sarah adjusted her purse strap over her shoulder. "My office is in that building, not their downtown location."

"That area built up fast, didn't it?"

"Yes, Sioux Falls's landscape keeps growing and growing."

"Maybe if you stop by tomorrow night you'd—"

The door buzzer sounded, interrupting Mark. Sarah

turned to see a frazzled-looking woman rush into the store.

Mark stepped around the cutting counter. "May I help you?"

"Thank goodness you're still open. Do you carry crochet thread? One of my children just told me they need it for a project at school tomorrow."

"I have a small supply over here because some quilters use it to tie their quilts together." Mark pointed to an area that held various types of thread.

He turned to Sarah with an apologetic expression, as if he'd broken a date, not left a thought dangling.

Sarah waved him off with her hand. "I'm sure I'll see you tomorrow. Good night."

"Good night." Mark's eyes held hers for precious seconds before he turned to follow his customer. Had disappointment flickered in his eyes? She'd been reluctant to leave, and now that reluctance was magnified by the emotion Mark conveyed with his eyes. Had he wanted to tell her something important?

Even though she didn't want to, Sarah knew it was time to go. It was too late to choose fabric, Mark had a customer, and he needed to close the store. Pivoting on one heel, Sarah turned and walked to the exit. She pushed through the door, triggering the buzzer that became muffled by the traffic noise as she crossed the threshold.

Pressing her key fob, her compact's headlights welcomed her as she walked toward the parking space. Once she opened her car door she couldn't resist one last glance at Mark through the plate-glass windows of Granny Bea's.

To her surprise he stood by the door, visiting with

Caroline and Rodney but watching her. He lifted a hand and waved good-bye.

She'd definitely stop by Granny Bea's to purchase her fabric tomorrow night. Slipping into her car, Sarah began to choose or eliminate outfits that she could wear tomorrow, a mental activity that still occupied her thoughts when she arrived home.

Sarah managed to make the early bird Bible study at church even though she changed outfits three times before leaving her house. She'd settled on a short-sleeved royal-blue sheath that she accessorized with a black-, royal-, and white-striped silk scarf. Her black pumps polished her look and added height to her five-foot frame. Her wardrobe indecisions left her feeling rushed, and she couldn't shake it even though she'd pulled into the office parking lot with minutes to spare.

As Sarah walked toward the entrance, the mock-cherry trees surrounding the office building greeted her with their soft pink flowers. The light spring breeze wafted the petals' fragrance through the air, and their pollen-filled centers buzzed with activity.

She entered the building and unlocked her office door. The plush carpet cushioned each step as she walked across the short space to her cherrywood desk. After dropping her tote bag onto her office chair, she hurried to the adjacent room and worked her way down the wall lined with office equipment. She turned on the photocopy machine before checking the fax for any messages received after business hours. She straightened the staplers, paper-clip holders, and pens on the counter then readied the postage meter for use that day.

The workroom doubled as a kitchenette. Once the

business machines were ready, Sarah turned to the opposite wall and prepared a pot of coffee. Her company provided a photocopier, postage meter, conference room, coffeemaker, and a vending area for the business suites housed down the hall from her office. Of course, the cost to use the office machines was in addition to their rent, but for some start-up businesses this was a very attractive service since it kept their equipment costs down.

Sarah usually arrived about fifteen minutes early to get these tasks completed before the eight o'clock workday started for her clients. She had barely gotten everything up and running and her tote bag and purse into her desk drawer when Ashley Vetter burst through the door.

"Is the coffee ready?" Ashley stopped short and teetered on her stiletto heels. She inhaled. "It is. Remember those case study articles I told you about? My deadline is today at noon, and I was up half the night trying to finish them. I'm not complaining. Those writing gigs are paying the bills while I get established and start attracting clients. I just need to stop procrastinating until my deadlines."

"I think you mean socializing."

Ashley grinned over her shoulder as she strode toward the workroom.

Sarah followed her and stopped beside the coffeepot. "Has any of your advertising worked?" she asked. Ashley's lease was the first one Sarah landed in her building manager position, so she hoped Ashley's business would succeed.

"Not yet, but I am networking." Ashley poured the fresh coffee into Sarah's cup and then into her own insulated mug. She stuck the pot back on the heating element and clicked the lid on her cup. "People have told me that I'm crazy to be a freelance paralegal, but I want to be my own boss. Last night at the chamber event I think I made some good contacts. Plus I met a really cute guy."

Fresh out of college, Ashley had an idealistic outlook on life in general. "You seem to meet a cute guy once a week." Sarah laughed but she could see why the tall, lithe, and leggy Ashley was so popular.

Ashley shrugged her shoulders. "Well, as you know, most of them don't amount to more than one date. You're always so great to listen to my lovelorn tales." She put her arm over her face in fake distress. She peeked under her arm. "*Lovelorn* is an expression from your generation, right?" Her lips curled into a sly smile.

"Aren't you the funny one this morning. You know it's a little before my time." Sarah grinned before she took a sip of coffee.

Ashley leaned against the countertop in front of the coffeepot. "I hope this latest guy calls like he said he would. Not only is he cute, but he seemed to have substance, and I caught him glancing my way from time to time. That's usually a good indication that he's interested."

"Do you really think so?" Sarah sat down on a folding chair beside a small table. She smiled, remembering several of Mark's lingering looks the night before.

Ashley wrinkled her brow and narrowed her eyes. "Your voice sounds, I don't know, dreamy. Sarah, are you holding out on me? Is there a man in your life?"

Since she wasn't able to ask Karla's advice, maybe she should bounce it off Ashley. She'd been dying to talk about Mark. The occasional glances her way that turned into longer looks. The way his eyes shone when he looked at her. Feelings of happiness wanted to bubble out; still, she held them in.

Ashley's laugh bounced around the room. "There is someone. You're blushing just thinking about him."

"Well, there's someone I'm interested in, and I think he's interested in me, but I don't know for sure." Adolescent feelings of insecurity rushed back. She'd been younger than Ashley the last time she felt this way about a guy.

"Spill it, girlfriend." Ashley sipped her coffee.

Sarah hesitated. Ashley was almost twenty years her junior. Sarah had been a bad judge of character at that age.

"Is he someone in the building?" Ashley raised her eyebrows, prompting Sarah to answer.

"No." Sarah shook her head with more force than necessary, causing her dangly earrings to bounce against her jawbone. Somehow it didn't seem ethical to date one of her tenants.

Raising her cup and taking another sip of coffee, Ashley held Sarah's gaze. "Then who?" she asked, lowering her cup.

Sarah cleared her throat. She had to tell someone, and Ashley had confided in her. "His name is Mark Sanders, and he runs Granny Bea's quilt shop."

"That's why you enrolled in quilting lessons!" Ashley smiled wide.

"Kind of." Sarah shrugged but knew her own smile matched Ashley's. She'd save the other reason for another conversation.

Ashley made no move to head to her office. "Tell me about him."

Sarah checked her watch. She still had a few minutes until her official start time. "He's close to my age with brown hair."

"And?"

"He's about five foot eight or nine, wide shoulders, stocky frame."

Ashley kept smiling. "Is he cute?" Her voice raised a few octaves as she said the word *cute*.

"Yes." A thrill ran through Sarah, raising her voice to the same height as Ashley's. It felt good to express her feelings.

"So, I take it since you know his name, you've spoken with him." Ashley took another sip of her coffee.

"Of course, several times but nothing much more than small talk. However, I've caught him looking at me and his gaze lingers, and—" a flush crept onto Sarah's cheeks "—when he demonstrated a sewing machine, he held my hand to guide me through one of the instructions." The skin on Sarah's hand where Mark had touched her tingled. She shrugged. "I don't know, though. Maybe it's just me hoping I have the same effect on him as he does on me."

Ashley rolled her eyes. "Women know when a man's interested. We just need reassurance from our friends. You consider me a friend, right?"

Sarah nodded. The click of a door handle cut through the silence.

"Sarah?" Karla's footsteps padded across the carpet.

"In here," Sarah called.

Ashley straightened. "Time to get to work." She walked toward the door and nodded a greeting to Karla, who stood just outside the threshold. Ashley paused at the doorway and turned. "Sarah, he's interested in you."

In the second it took Ashley to disappear down the hall, Karla's jaw dropped. Her astonished expression caused Sarah's heart to plummet to her stomach. "Who's interested?"

Lifting her cup to her lips, Sarah gulped the last of her coffee, stalling for time.

As Sarah polished off the coffee, Karla crossed her arms over her chest and pursed her lips in disgust.

Sarah waved a dismissive hand in the air as she stood. "Nothing really."

The raised eyebrow and glaring stare told Sarah that Karla wasn't buying that explanation.

"Ashley and I were just trading girl talk about guys we've recently met and the signals they send that shows they're interested." Sarah smiled at Karla as she squeezed past her and walked over to her desk.

"When did you meet a guy?" Karla followed Sarah and seated herself in a guest chair.

Easing down in her office chair, Sarah slipped on her phone earpiece. "I met him while I was shopping." She tried to keep her tone casual, not filled with the giddiness she'd let slip when talking with Ashley about Mark.

"So, you're picking guys up at the mall now?" The sarcasm oozed from Karla's remark.

"No, I'm not picking up guys at the mall. Actually, you more than anyone know that I've never picked up a guy in my life." Sarah's response was clipped because she was tired of Karla's attitude.

Karla shrugged. "The old Sarah wouldn't have, but now it's like I don't know you anymore since your diagnosis."

I could say the same about you.

"Why didn't you tell me?" Karla leaned forward in her chair.

Sarah sighed. "I planned to talk to you about this last night but—"

"We had more serious matters to discuss," Karla interrupted. "That's why I'm here. I don't think you fully understand my concern for you."

Sarah's shoulder's tightened. The tension crept up her neck. She rested her right elbow on her desk and massaged the muscles over that shoulder blade. The last thing she needed today was to deal with numbness in her right arm. She was so tired of this same conversation with Karla. Not to mention this wasn't the appropriate time or place to have it *again*. "I understand your concern."

"I don't think you do," Karla interjected. "You don't take anything I say seriously." She scooted to the edge of her chair and rested her forearms on her knees. "I searched MS and discovered it makes you fatigued. You need to rest. You're doing too much. A new job. A new hobby. And now I find out a new boyfriend." Karla rolled her eyes.

"Enough." Sarah raised her voice and rolled her right shoulder to keep the muscles loose. "This conversation is over. If you haven't noticed, I am at work. You might not think I need to work but I do. I'm managing my fatigue with medicine and it's working." *Most of the time*. Sarah paused, not for drama but to calm the burning anger her friend ignited.

"I'm very sorry to say this—" Sarah's voice now non-confrontational "—but unless you want to rent office space, you're going to have to leave. I have work to do."

Karla practically jumped out of her chair. "You're

kicking me out?" She grabbed her purse and huffed over to the door. She opened it, paused, then glanced over her shoulder, all traces of her anger gone. "Sarah, be careful," she said, her tone now conversational. "Most guys have a hard time committing to a healthy woman, much less one who has to deal with health issues on a daily basis. I know you don't believe me, but I have your best interests at heart." With a small shrug of her shoulders and a weak smile, Karla closed the door behind her.

Every car that pulled into a parking space caught Mark's eye. He'd been watching for a familiar black compact since five o'clock even though he knew if Sarah worked eight to five it'd take a good half hour or longer to get to Granny Bea's through the rush-hour traffic.

Mark replayed their conversation from the previous night as he reshelved bolts of material. He was certain she said she'd stop by after work, but six o'clock came and went. Still no Sarah.

Ding-dong. Mark jerked his head up, hoping it was Sarah that walked through the door. Disappointment tamped out his initial hope.

"What brings you to my store?" Mark pushed a bolt of fabric into place as he tried to get a grip on his feelings.

"It's that time of the year again." Diane Wall held up a large manila envelope. "How have you been?"

Mark met her halfway in the main aisle of the store. He admired the cut of her expensive business suit as he extended his hand. "Great. Once a sharp dresser, always a sharp dresser. You've never looked better."

Diane smiled at his compliment and shook the hand

he offered. "Thank you. As cochair of the MS walk, I'm dropping your packet off for—" she tilted her head as she read the team's name written in black marker on the outside of the envelope "—Gert's Gang. I'm glad you continue to do this each year in honor of your mom."

"Well—" Mark took the information and peeked in at the contents "—old habits die hard, I guess." He'd considered stopping when his mom passed away, but she'd provided such a good life for him, all on her own, he decided to honor her memory by continuing to raise money to fight the disease that left her a struggling single mom.

"I guess." Diane shrugged. She twisted the pointed toe of her shoe. "I'm glad you're doing okay."

"Thanks." Mark knew that when Diane broke it off with him six months ago that she really thought they'd get back together. "How are things going for you?"

Diane held up her left hand and wiggled her ring finger. A large princess-cut diamond sparkled under the fluorescent store lights.

"Congratulations." His dating theory did work— she'd found her true love.

"Thank you." Diane held her hand out and admired her ring. "Well," she said, putting her hand down, "I'm sure I'll see you at the walk." She headed to the exit, her high heels clicking on the polished gray tiled floor.

Mark folded the flap of the envelope closed and held it between his fingers. "Thanks again for dropping this off." He walked to the cash register.

Diane stopped and glanced over her shoulder. "Are you seeing anyone special?"

Mark shrugged. Diane shook her head and pushed

through the door. She held it open so another customer could enter. Relief swirled through Mark.

"Thanks." Sarah smiled her gratitude to the woman then snagged a cart and stashed her purse where a child should sit.

"There you are. I thought you were going to be a no-show." Mark greeted Sarah with a wide smile.

Pushing the cart with a slow pace, Sarah stopped in front of the cash register. "I made up some time at work."

"Long day?" Mark asked. Although Sarah's attire remained wrinkle-free, her body seemed to have lost its starch. It looked as if it took all her energy to take the next step. Instead of maintaining her usually erect posture, she leaned on the cart. Dullness replaced the usual sparkle in her eyes.

"That is an understatement." She raised tired eyes to meet his. "How was your day?"

"Pretty busy up until an hour ago." Mark tapped the envelope on the counter by the cash register to give his hands something to do. "Unhappy renter? Would it help to talk about it? I'm a good listener."

A slight twinkle appeared in Sarah's eyes at his offer. "It was a personal matter, nothing to do with work." She sighed, her mouth turning into a frown. "I'm pretty sure a longtime friendship is ending."

He knew it. A bad breakup. He could read the signs from a mile away. Who would let a good-looking lady like Sarah get away? *I would.* Mark sobered at the thought that was surely brought on by Diane's visit. "That happens sometimes."

"I guess." Sarah shrugged with what looked like great effort.

Mark could fix this. Maybe not tonight, but in the near future. He'd bring her self-confidence back so she could go out and face the dating world and find the elusive fairy tale all women seemed to believe in as exampled by Diane's recent engagement. She'd apparently found true love.

"Well, you're here now, and among friends, well, friend." Mark grinned.

Sarah managed a crooked smile. Some of the normal sparkle returned to her coal-colored eyes. "Yes, I am." She sighed. "I should probably pick out my fabric."

Mark abandoned the envelope beside the cash register and rounded the end of the counter. "Mind if I tag along while you pick out your material?"

"Company would be nice. I could use a distraction." Sarah's stance straightened as she pushed the cart, but her pace remained slow as she made her way down an aisle.

Her flowery fragrance lured Mark closer to the cart as they walked to the back corner of the quilt shop. "Are you making a wall quilt or table runner?" As they passed by the section with heavier-weight material, Mark straightened a bolt of denim someone had pulled forward.

"I planned on a wall quilt, but since I might be doing all the sewing by hand, I'm thinking maybe I should go with the table runner." Sarah stopped the cart in front of patterned cotton fabric.

"What did I tell you?" Mark waited for Sarah to look at him. "You can use my extra machines anytime."

"I know." Sarah pulled the paper with fabric requirements for the class from her purse. "And that's very generous of you, but…" Sarah's voice trailed off.

"No buts about it. Those machines sit in the work-room and only get used during quilting class, so don't worry about it."

Sarah pulled her pretty mouth into a pucker. Was she considering his offer to use the machines or thinking about telling him to back off? Her grip tightened on the cart. "Here's the thing. Will it really help to use the machines, if I don't know how to sew? I mean, I don't want to ruin my fabric, ripping out mistakes."

Mark crossed his arms over his chest and rocked back on his heels. "I see your point."

"So it's settled. I'll sew my quilt by hand and make the table runner."

"Hmm. Tell you what." Mark dropped his arms and crossed the sales floor to a book display. He couldn't let her get out of coming into the quilt store so easily. He pulled out a hardbound book and returned to the spot where Sarah stood. "I happen to have in my pos-session a manual on sewing basics." He held it out for Sarah to see.

Sarah took the book and turned it over. Her eyes fo-cused on the bottom left-hand corner.

"You don't have to buy it. Use it when you come into the store to practice on the sewing machines. And you can practice on remnant fabric."

"You're making it hard for a girl to say no." Sarah lifted her turmoil-filled eyes to search his face. It ap-peared as if she wanted to say yes, but something was keeping her from it, something other than the fact that she lacked sewing skills.

The last thing he wanted to do was scare her away. "I'm just saying, if you want a wall quilt, make one.

Don't let a tiny obstacle like not having expert sewing skills get in the way."

Sarah laughed. "Tiny obstacle?"

Mark shrugged. "It's all a matter of perspective."

For a few seconds Sarah drew her brows together, and then a smile lit her face. "Okay, I'm convinced. I'll make the wall quilt." She handed the book back to Mark.

The jangle of the door alerted Mark to another customer. He shelved the sewing book and greeted his customer. By the time he turned his attention back to Sarah, she and her fabric bolts were waiting patiently by the cutting center.

"Ready?" Mark slid a bolt of light blue paisley fabric toward him.

"Yes." Sarah ran her finger down the paper with the fabric requirements for the wall quilt. "I need three yards of that one."

Mark flipped the bolt over several times, releasing the tightly bound fabric before he grabbed the cut end of the cloth and stretched a length of material over the yardstick attached to the Formica-topped cutting counter. His sharp shears whooshed down the material, cutting it loose from the bolt.

"A yard of each of the light blue and white." Sarah pushed the solid bolts of cotton to Mark.

"This will make a pretty quilt. The paisley's the back and part of the block pattern, right?"

Sarah nodded her head. "Is that the name of the fabric's pattern—paisley? I just thought it was tear shaped and fitting for a Job's Tears quilt."

"Guess I never saw that in the paisley pattern. But

you're right. Some of the print is tear shaped." Mark slid the cut fabric to the side. "That it?"

"No." Sarah handed Mark another bolt. It was from the clearance area with preprinted Christmas pillow panels. "The printed instructions on the fabric make this pillow project sound easy. Would a project like this help me learn to sew?"

"It would." Mark cut on the solid black line to cut the panel from the bolt.

"When is a good night for me to come in and practice?" Sarah's eyes shone in spite of the dark circles that underscored them.

He bowled tomorrow, and Friday at four started the first weekend he'd had off in six weeks. Mark wanted to be in the store when Sarah came in to practice.

"Monday?" Some of the glow started to diminish from Sarah's face. Mark added hurriedly, "I'm sure you're busy Friday night."

"No." Sarah shook her head.

"Friday it is." Mark didn't really have any plans anyway. He could hang around the store.

Chapter 3

Mark sat in his office, surfing the internet, when the workroom illuminated. He swiveled in his chair and caught a glimpse of Sarah through the glass window. Dressed in hip-hugger jeans and a white T-shirt, she carried a denim tote bag. Sarah walked to the demonstration machine Mark showed her how to work on Tuesday night.

Sarah laid her tote bag on the table and studied the sewing machine. She reached a finger out and touched the power button. Light reflected on the arm of the sewing machine, and Sarah pulled a fist back and forth in a victory fashion.

When she looked up, Mark waved. Sarah wiggled her fingers. Her sheepish smile conveyed her embarrassment at being caught celebrating her success at remembering how to turn on the sewing machine.

Mark rounded the corner of the door. "Hi."

Sarah giggled. "No one was supposed to see that."

"What else do you remember?" Mark watched the extra flush on Sarah's cheeks brighten the sparkle in her eyes as he crossed the room. No sign of the smudges of darkness that half-mooned her eyes on Wednesday.

Sarah lowered to the chair. "This is where I choose the stitch I want to sew with and this—" Sarah expertly lifted the lever behind the arm of the sewing machine "—lifts the presser foot."

"A quick learner."

"Remembering how to work the machine isn't really sewing." Sarah gave the machine a good once-over. "For example, how do you make it work after you turn it on?"

They hadn't gotten that far the other night. "You run the machine with the foot feed on the floor, or some people put it beside the machine and use their forearm. Would you like me to demonstrate the machine for you?"

"I would, but do you have time? I don't want to take you away from your business."

"Actually, my sales floor shift ended at four. I stuck around to do some special orders." Not a lie. He'd placed two special orders while he waited for Sarah to arrive. Mark held up a finger. "I'll be back in a minute."

On the sales floor, Mark grabbed some lavender fabric from the remnant bin and a spool of black thread. He'd found when demonstrating the machines that dark thread on light fabric allowed the customer a better view of the stitches.

"Mark, didn't you want to take this to your office?" Terri, one of his part-timers, held the MS envelope in the air.

"Thanks." Mark took the envelope from Terri.

Back in the workroom, Sarah had apparently pulled her Christmas project out of her tote bag while she waited for Mark to return.

"Do you have scissors in your bag?" Mark asked, dropping the envelope on the front table.

"Yes." Sarah peeked in her bag and retrieved them.

"We'll practice on this fabric." Mark took the scissors Sarah offered. He cut the wrapper off the lavender material then scooted another chair close to the sewing machine and patted the seat. "Mind switching?"

"Not at all." Sarah slid from one chair seat to the other.

Once seated, Mark ripped the cellophane covering off the spool of thread. "This is how you thread this machine." Aware of his adeptness at this task, Mark took his time putting the thread on the spool holder and pulling it through the necessary path to the needle.

Sarah stood so she could have a clearer view. "Looks easy enough." She smiled at Mark.

"Since you just want to practice a straight stitch, that's all I'm going to show you."

Sarah leaned forward and peered around Mark. "That is the stitch the machine is set to sew." The light scent of her perfume teased him to move closer.

"See, you are a quick learner." Mark closed his eyes and breathed deeply, filling his memory with the flowery scent. Sarah's scent.

Sarah sat back, and the pleasant fragrance drifted away from him. Mark wanted to follow the fading bouquet the same way hungry cartoon characters used to follow an animated cloud of food aroma into trouble.

As if on cue, Mark's stomach rumbled. He cleared his throat. "Excuse me."

"Am I keeping you from your dinner?"

"Not really, I just had an early lunch." Mark reached for the lavender cotton material. A long, low growl cut through the silence in the room.

Sarah placed her hand on his, stopping his movement. "Mark, you're hungry. You don't have to stay and demonstrate the machine. I'll get the manual and try to figure it out myself."

Her concern showed not only on her face but in her voice. It melted Mark's heart. Why would any man lucky enough to be Sarah's type break it off with her? Anger toward her unknown ex-boyfriend sparked in Mark. The unexpected emotion shocked him back to the moment.

"I'm serious." Sarah's silky hand patted his before pulling away.

"Okay, I admit it. I'm hungry but…" He should have run out for an afternoon snack before she arrived. He didn't want to leave to go get dinner now because it was evident that Sarah planned to stay and practice. How would he explain leaving and coming back when he already told her that his shift had ended? Plus on Wednesday night he'd intended to ask her to dinner, but his last-minute customer had interrupted and Mark had lost his nerve.

"But what? I'm sure I can figure this out." Doubt flickered through Sarah's dark eyes as her gaze left his and rested on the sewing machine.

"I promised to help you." Mark didn't intend on breaking this promise. After all, Sanders men only broke big promises, not little ones. "Have you eaten dinner yet?"

"No." Sarah never took her eyes off the sewing machine.

"I could order a pizza." Mark hoped Sarah would go for his idea. "We could continue the demonstration while we wait for it to be delivered."

Happiness skipped through Mark's heart when Sarah's eyes met his and she nodded. "I'd like that."

The squeak of the folding chair's legs reverberated through the room as Mark stood. "What do you like on your pizza?"

"Anything and everything."

"I'll be right back." With a quick flick of his wrist, Mark pulled the thread off the sewing machine and handed it to Sarah. "Try rethreading the machine while I'm gone. If you succeed, go ahead and celebrate."

Sarah gave him a lopsided grin as she took the thread.

Once back in his office, Mark, looking through the wall window, watched Sarah thread the machine as he ordered the pizza. When she looked up and saw that he was watching, she smirked, fisted her hand, and pulled it back in victory. Mark erupted in laughter, confusing the pizza place employee on the other end of the line.

Mark came back into the workroom. "Pizza is ordered." He checked the machine. "Victory celebration deserved. Now I'll show you how to wind the bobbin."

By the time the pizza was delivered, Sarah had practiced sewing a straight stitch several times. Mark placed the pizza on the first table in the workroom, along with two cans of soda and napkins.

"I think I'll do a few more practice runs then start on my pillow." Sarah moved from the folding chair in front of the sewing machine to a folding chair across the table from Mark.

He lifted the lid of the pizza box.

"That smells great. What'd you order?"

"All meat." Mark used a plastic fork to serve Sarah a piece of pizza. She placed it in front of her then clasped her hands and lowered her eyes. Mark hadn't prayed before meals since his mom passed away. Not because he wasn't a believer. He'd just gotten out of the habit. Following Sarah's good example, Mark bowed his head.

Thank You, Lord, for this nourishment and the blessings of new friends. Amen.

That felt good. He'd have to remember to say grace more often. Mark lifted his eyes to find Sarah patiently waiting for him to finish.

She smiled. "Next time we'll have to say grace out loud." She lifted her pizza to her lips.

Mark retrieved a piece of pizza for himself. *Next time.* That was a good sign.

"What's Gert's Gang?"

He raised his eyebrows in question as he chewed a bite of pizza. Had he been daydreaming and lost a thread of conversation?

Sarah used her pizza slice like a pointer, motioning toward the envelope lying on the table.

"Oh." Mark sipped his soda before he continued. "That's a team packet for the MS walk. My mom had MS. A few relatives and friends still participate to raise money in her honor. Her name's Gertrude Sanders."

"Your mom had MS."

Sarah's comment was barely audible. Or was it a question? Mark couldn't tell. Her eyes focused on the envelope, and her expression sobered.

"Pardon me?" Mark searched Sarah's face as she turned her attention back to him.

She cleared her throat. "You said she *had* MS."

"She passed away two years ago from—" Mark looked down, breaking Sarah's compassion-filled gaze "—natural causes."

"I'm sorry." Mark's forearm warmed where Sarah rested her palm.

"Thank you." He lifted his eyes.

Sarah patted his arm. "Tell me about her."

Disbelief swirled through Mark. None of the other women he'd dated since his mother's death had asked that question. They talked about themselves, and he let them. It was all part of his dating system.

"It's okay if you're not ready." Sarah had apparently mistaken his silence as reluctance.

"No, it's okay. I don't mind talking about her." Mark smiled. Sometimes Sarah reminded him of his mom. Not in looks or stature but in her gentle caring way. The Christian way, his mom always said—putting others first.

Sarah slid a slice of pizza from the box and offered it to Mark. His previous thought and her action widened his smile.

"We moved in with my grandma Bea when I was five, and Mom opened a tailor and sewing business in the basement. She was a good seamstress, and it didn't take long until she had quite a clientele list."

The lilt of Sarah's laughter filled the room. "I'm sorry to interrupt, but no wonder you looked so shocked when I said I didn't know how to sew." The crinkles around Sarah's eyes deepened when she laughed, and merriment shone from her dark eyes.

Mark chuckled. "I have to admit most of the women I grew up around sewed—my grandma, my mom, our neighbors Caroline and her mom. I was literally surrounded."

"Is that why you run a fabric and quilt shop? Because of the ladies in your life?"

"Actually, I inherited it from Mom. When her tailoring business grew, she opened a fabric store."

"Where did the quilting come in?" Sarah crinkled her napkin in her fist and lifted her soda can.

"Mom decided she needed a quiet hobby to help her cope with her MS. She ended up with lots of scrap fabric from her tailoring business, so she began quilting."

Sarah's eyes widened, then she began to cough. She lowered the soda can and covered her mouth with her napkin.

"Are you okay?" Mark pushed his chair back and started to rise.

"I'm fine." Sarah spoke through the napkin. "Just went down wrong."

"Are you sure?"

Sarah nodded. Mark lowered to the chair.

"Do you mind my asking, how old your mom was when she was diagnosed with MS?"

"Not at all. Twenty-five. Tell me about your parents." Mark grabbed another piece of pizza from the box.

"They live in Brookings. Dad's a retired professor at South Dakota State University and Mom's a legal secretary. Three more years and she'll retire, too. Believe me, she's counting the days. They plan to do a lot of traveling."

"Good for them."

"I think so, too. My older brother and his family live in California. Do you have siblings?"

Mark shook his head as he stood. "Would you like any more pizza?"

"No, thank you."

He closed the lid on the pizza box and slid it to the end of the table. "I'll put it here so I remember to take it home." He gathered their used napkins and the soda cans and walked to the waste can.

"What's your dad like?"

Mark stopped midstep. He never got used to answering this question. He turned and shrugged. "I don't know. He left when I was five."

Sarah leaned back to avoid the steam as she poured boiling water into her china teapot. In seconds the clear water turned pale brown and fragrant as the liquid released the flavors and aroma of the dried tea leaves. Her mom would be here any minute with their once-a-week calorie splurge—bakery cinnamon rolls.

After transferring a wicker tray filled with her pansy-patterned tea service from the counter to the kitchen table, Sarah yawned and stretched. She'd spent a fitful night reliving her question to Mark. Not because of the answer she'd received when she asked about his dad— that he'd deserted his family. It was the timing involved.

It didn't take a genius to do the math. His dad must've left the same time Mark's mom was diagnosed with multiple sclerosis. Karla's cruel remark about men not committing to a woman with health problems had instantly echoed through her mind at Mark's admission. Karla's haunting statement kept Sarah wary of her and Mark's actions the remainder of the night. Was it flirting or friendly banter? She didn't want to mislead him like she'd been misled so many years ago. When she told him that she had MS, would he prove Karla right? Would his interest in her wane?

"I hope not. I like Mark." Happiness tickled her heart at her verbal acknowledgment.

Sarah smiled and traced the lettering on the Granny Bea's bag lying on the table. She trusted God just like Job had, that good could come out of her situation, and that might include Mark. She hoped it included Mark.

The roar of a car engine overtook the chirping birds and neighborhood sounds filtering through the open kitchen window, announcing her mom's arrival. Sarah opened the back door and waved a welcome to her mother.

Dressed in skinny jeans and a long blue T-shirt, her mom appeared ten years younger than her actual age. She pecked Sarah's cheek as she passed through the doorway. "How are you, dear?"

"Fine, a little tired. I didn't sleep well last night." Sarah looked down at her grungy but comfortable exercise outfit, wishing she'd inherited her mom's casual dress style. Sarah closed the door and took a seat at the table.

"Is it from your MS?" Her mother set the bakery box in the center of the table, slid her purse from her shoulder, and stashed it on an empty chair as she sat across the table from Sarah.

"No, something was bothering me. But if I don't take a nap the loss of sleep might aggravate my symptoms."

"I worry that you're doing too much." Her mom added a lump of sugar to each cup and poured the hot tea over it.

Sarah reached for the saucer and carefully placed it in front of her. "Not you, too." Sarah punctuated her sentence with a sigh as she reached over and snagged a cinnamon roll.

Her mother scooted back into her chair. "What do you mean?"

Sarah leaned forward, resting her elbow on the table and her chin in her hand. "Karla's against my job, my hobby, and…"

Her mother's raised eyebrows prompted Sarah to continue.

"My interest in a gentleman." Sarah pinched a bite off the cinnamon roll and nibbled on it while she watched her mother's reaction.

Her mother pursed her lips and narrowed her eyes. "We'll get back to him later. How against everything is Karla?"

"Enough that it's straining our relationship."

"That's too bad. You've been friends since kindergarten. Is it really a strain or just a difference of opinion?"

Sarah watched her mother bite into her roll. "It's a vehement difference of opinion, and she just won't let the subject matter die. She wants me to agree with her and I can't. She thinks I shouldn't be working and wants me to quit my job."

"Well—" her mother nodded her head "—she has a valid point there. It's stressful and tiring learning a new job. You should have considered that when you were searching for a different career."

"What?" Although every fiber of her being wanted to jump up from her chair, Sarah remained seated. "You agree with Karla?" Her tone reflected her outrage; then it clicked. Sarah narrowed her eyes. "Did Karla call you?"

Her mother held up her palm. "Hear me out. She's concerned about you, and so am I. You should have looked for part-time office work so you'd have more time to rest."

"I already have too much free time to think about my future with MS. That's why I took up quilting, to occupy my mind with something other than my illness." Sarah took a drink of her tea. The lukewarm liquid did little to calm the anger shaking her insides.

"I don't understand why Karla's upset by that one. It's a nice sedentary activity."

Sarah rolled her eyes and pushed her roll away, no longer excited for her weekly treat. "I didn't choose quilting because it was sedentary. I wanted to create something beautiful. I think you and Karla should attend one of my MS support groups. They encourage you to remain active as long as possible."

Her mother answered with a shrug then sipped her tea. "Now, what's this about a love interest?"

"He's not a love interest." *Just a possibility.* "Mark is an acquaintance that I'm getting to know better."

"Well, don't rush into anything." Her mother's features softened as she reached across the table and clasped Sarah's hand. "Promise me that you'll really get to know him before you get involved."

"I promise." She'd never repeat her past mistake when it came to love.

"And be honest about your MS." Her mom pulled her hand away.

Sarah sighed then nodded.

"I'm your mother, and I love you and don't want

to see you hurt. Now probably isn't the best time to get involved with someone. Some men can't handle being a caregiver, at any age." Concern shone in her mother's eyes.

Maybe "some men," but Mark seemed different. After all, he helped his mother. Sarah looked at the Granny Bea's bag at the other end of the table. She'd been drawn to the Job's Tears quilt pattern because she wanted a visual reminder that if you accepted the good from God, you must accept the bad. She hadn't planned the people closest to her would expect her to give up, just like Job's friends and family.

Mark squinted to read the thread number on the end of the spool. *Probably should invest in some cheap readers.* He pushed the thread into the display holder. First his hairline receded, now his eyesight was getting bad. What would be next—his knees?

On Saturday afternoon, he'd toyed with the idea of calling Sarah for a last-minute date. The gorgeous April temperatures beckoned him outside. He'd heard the falls were rushing from the spring snowmelt and thought maybe Sarah would like to take a walk through Falls Park with him. She'd listed her phone number on the class registration, but that was for emergencies, like a class cancellation. In the end, Mark felt it might be an unethical use of the form. Besides, it was easier to say no over the phone, so he planned to ask her tomorrow night before or after class, whichever time worked better.

The jangle of the door buzzer echoed through the room. "Be with you in a minute," Mark called as he shelved another spool of thread. He lifted the empty thread box and turned. Sarah stood at the end of the aisle.

Delight replaced Mark's dismay of the aging process from seconds ago.

"Hi. I came to practice before tomorrow night." Apprehension dotted Sarah's features as she held up her tote bag. "I'm going to start my pillow."

The soft pink blouse she wore complemented the rosy glow of her skin. The hoops of her dangly earrings and sandal straps matched the color of her shirt, dressing up her denim crop pants.

"As good as you did on Friday night, I'm sure you'll finish the pillow tonight." He used the empty box to motion toward the back of the store. "After you."

"I don't really think I'll need your help tonight." Sarah glanced over her shoulder.

Mark's balloon of happiness popped. He liked being in the same room as Sarah. He liked being able to help her learn something new. He liked being needed.

"That didn't sound quite right. I appreciate the instructions you gave me on Friday." Sarah stopped in the darkened workroom doorway and turned to face Mark. "I'd just like to try this on my own tonight." Her voice held a determination that didn't match her expression.

"Excuse me." Mark reached around Sarah and flicked the light switch. He momentarily closed his eyes to savor her flowery perfume before backing up to allow her entry into the room. "You want to test your skill?"

"Exactly." Sarah smiled. "I feel confident when you're right beside me, but you won't be in class with me tomorrow night."

Mark followed Sarah into the workroom. "I understand." He did, too, but that didn't stop the searing disappointment of not being able to stay close to Sarah. Have a conversation with her. Ask her out. Mark watched Sarah turn on the sewing machine and pull her project from her bag.

Aware of his hesitation, he turned to take the box to the garbage can when he saw the Gert's Gang envelope that he'd forgotten to take home. He walked over to the table and picked it up.

"Mark." Sarah stepped closer to the table. "I meant to ask you the other night if you accept new members in Gert's Gang. I'm going to participate in the MS walk and thought it might be more fun to have people to walk with."

"Sure! The more the merrier." Joy fueled Mark's exuberant response. Why hadn't he thought of inviting her to join their group last Friday night? This meant more time to spend with Sarah. Mark opened the envelope to pull out an individual pledge sheet.

"Thanks for doing this, Sarah." He handed her the paper. "The money that walkers bring in goes a long way in helping with MS research."

"That's good." Sarah took the offered paper. "I have a personal interest in multiple sclerosis."

"Me, too, but you already know that." Mark smiled at Sarah.

"Do you mind if I ask you another question about your mom?" Sarah's dangly earrings swayed with a slight tilt of her head.

"Not at all." Mark put the envelope and box on the table. He crossed his arms over his chest and rocked back on his heels.

"How did MS affect your mom's quality of life? Obviously, she worked." Sarah looked around the room. "But did she work full-time?"

As soon as she asked the question, Sarah's stance changed. Oddly, she looked braced, as if she expected Mark to deliver devastating news.

"Yes, she did. Mom stayed very active despite her symptoms. They didn't have all the treatment options available then, either. She started a quilting circle at our church, was a room mother when I was in school, and was involved in a businesswoman's association, in addition to running the house and business." The more Mark talked the more elated Sarah appeared. She placed her hand over her heart and sighed. Her smile was so wide that it narrowed her eyes. Mark felt himself scowl at Sarah's strange reaction to his answer.

She didn't seem to notice. "That's wonderful." She looked at the ceiling and sighed again. "Just wonderful." Then she closed her eyes.

Aware that his scowl deepened, Mark quickly relaxed his face before Sarah opened her eyes. The last thing he wanted to do was offend her.

When Sarah opened her eyes, serenity replaced the apprehension that had lurked in her features. "That really is very encouraging to hear."

"Granny Bea and I did help her quite a bit, but she was very courageous handling her disease." *Unlike the coward who left her alone to struggle.* Mark caught himself before he snorted to emphasize his thought. That might be hard to explain to Sarah.

"She was lucky to have you two."

"Well—" Mark shrugged "—that's what family does, I guess." *Blood family, that is.* He hated thinking about the man that walked out on his mother when she needed

him the most. It reminded him that he was a Sanders
man and, if he was tested, might find out he had a yellow streak, too. A test Mark never planned to take.

"Are you okay?" Sarah's smile faded.

Mark pushed the depressing truth from his mind.
"Yes, it's just that some memories are not always good
ones."

Sarah shook her head absently, her dangly earrings
shimmering in the light. "I'm learning that."

Great. He'd made her think of her recent breakup.
He'd never understand why some guy would dump
Sarah. This was an excellent opportunity for him to
step in and start building her self-confidence. "Sarah,
I had a nice time on Friday night, and I was wondering
if you'd like to go out with me sometime." The practiced words tumbled out as nervous tension kicked in.
Why had that happened? Nerves never came into play
when he asked a lady out, because he never took it per-
sonally if she turned him down.

Sarah's eyes widened at the surprise turn in conversation. Her face softened and her eyes sparkled. "I'd
love to."

Who would give up a woman that beamed with happiness? "Great. Does Sunday afternoon work for you?"

"It does." Sarah affirmed her answer with a nod and
ran her fingers over the sign-up form she held.

"I almost forgot." Mark pointed to the paper. "Fill
that out and, as captain of the team, I'll give you a
packet for donations."

"Okay. Can I bring it back tomorrow night?" Sarah
studied the form.

"Sure. Do you mind if I ask you who it is you're
walking for?"

Sarah raised her eyes and stared straight into Mark's for a few seconds.

"I'm walking for me. I have MS."

Chapter 4

"I have MS." The quiet of the workroom ate up Sarah's admission, yet her words jumbled in Mark's mind as if he stood in a canyon, trying to decipher an echo.

Sarah has multiple sclerosis. The words started to register. Mark knew he should reach out to her. Pull her into a tight hug. Tell her everything would work out, but in true Sanders men fashion, his feet remained planted to the floor like a dead tree's roots in fertile soil.

Wide eyed, Sarah searched his face. He needed to say something to break the awkward silence that ensued after her statement. Should he say it'd be all right, when he knew the long, sometimes pain-filled road ahead of her?

Two deep lines formed between her brows. Panic forced the air from his lungs. No wonder she'd asked so many questions about his mother. How had he missed the signs?

Stupid question. He allowed himself to give in to attraction, that's how.

He hung his head. *Look at her.* He snapped his head back up. He didn't want her thinking that her disease made her unattractive because nothing could make Sarah unattractive. *Say something.*

"I'm, um, s-s-sorry to hear that."

Sarah blinked rapidly at his stammered response. He didn't see tears, but that was a sure sign they'd be coming. What would he do if she started to cry? He strained his ears, listening for the door buzzer. He needed a valid excuse, like a customer, to leave the room. His gut twisted. Why was he born a Sanders?

Sarah continued to frown; then she pulled her puckered mouth to the side as if she were contemplating a response.

Mark cleared his throat. He crossed his arms and rocked back on his heels. This time the Sanders genetics wouldn't win. He'd stay and face this difficult conversation. Mark forced reassurance into his voice.

"Sarah, I know your diagnosis may feel devastating, but they've made great medical strides in the treatment of MS, thanks to contributions from activities like this walk." He tapped his fingers on the heavy paper of the envelope. The contents rattled, emphasizing his point. "You'll have a better chance at managing the disease than my mom."

Sarah's gaze dropped to the envelope. She nodded before raising her eyes to his. Her black eyes bore into him. Could she see through his facade? That it was in his genetics to cut and run in times like these?

"And that's why it's great that you continue to support fund-raisers like the walk." Sarah smiled as she stepped closer. She laid her hand over his crossed arms. "I'm sorry that I dropped my diagnosis on you like that. I didn't even consider it might bring up memories of your mom."

What? She thought she'd hurt his feelings? The moisture that formed in her eyes wasn't from anguish over her diagnosis but empathy for him.

Sarah's kind words and silky touch started a reverberation deep in his heart.

"Don't be sorry." Emotion rasped his voice. He didn't deserve the apology. She did.

The jangle of the door announced the arrival of a customer. Sarah squeezed his forearm and slid her hand down his skin, releasing their contact. "I'd better get started on my project."

Mark nodded, not trusting his voice. His emotions had betrayed him once already. He turned and left the workroom.

As he walked to the cash register area, an older lady smiled his way. He watched his customer pick through the fat-quarter bin as Sarah's workroom confession played over and over in his mind like a skipped record.

"I have MS." "I have MS." He'd missed so many signs. The dark half-mooned eyes mirrored his mom's whenever she'd powered through the fatigue caused by the disease. The shuffling of Sarah's feet when she pushed the cart the other night. And then she thought—

"I'm ready to check out."

The impatient tone shocked Mark from his thoughts. The elderly lady stood in front of the cash register. Her pinched brows and pursed lips emphasized her irritation. How long had she stood right in front of him?

"Sorry." Mark pushed his thoughts of Sarah to the

back of his mind. He picked up the elderly woman's items that lay on the short counter, ready to be rung up.

Shaken by Sarah's revelation, he'd failed to greet this customer when he came back to the sales floor. Not good business. "Did you find everything all right?"

"I did."

"We have a new special on Tuesdays after five—buy one yard of clearance fabric, get the second yard half-price." Mark slipped a pink flyer advertising his Tuesday night special into his customer's bag as she swiped her card and entered her PIN.

The register spit out the store receipt. He handed it to the customer. "Thank you. Stop in again." He said the words automatically, knowing they were void of his usual sincerity when dealing with a store patron.

He pinched his eyes shut as the door jangled the customer's exit. Sarah's face filled his memory. Why did God keep striking good women with this disease? The concern she showed for him, although undeserved, twisted his heart. He should have been comforting her. He wanted to comfort her, but something held him back. Something beyond his control—his heritage. He clenched his fists in anger.

When he opened his eyes, Sarah stood beside the checkout counter.

"Don't let a cranky customer get to you." She pulled at her left earring and looked out the plate-glass window, trying to catch a glance of who might have been in the store.

Unbelievable that Sarah was worried about him. "It's not that." Mark shrugged. "Long day."

"Too long to give me your opinion?" Sarah smiled

as she held up a twelve-by-twelve square panel. "How'd I do?"

Mark took the fabric square from her. "Well, you sewed the right sides together and left an end open to stuff it. That's a good sign."

"Only because—" holding up numbered instructions that she'd cut from the panel, Sarah pointed and giggled "—the instructions show it that way. I'd never have given a thought as to which way the fabric should face when sewn together."

Mark chuckled. Sarah's face glowed with merriment as she admitted her ineptness as a seamstress.

"I wanted you to check my seams."

Mark whacked his head with his palm. "I forgot to show you how to follow the guide by the presser foot." He held the pillow top at eye level and inspected the seams.

"I followed the straight line on the fabric." Sarah pointed to a strip on the outside border of the printed picture of an old-fashioned ice-skating scene.

"Good job." Mark turned the square and looked at the next section. "Really, Sarah, you did well for your first time. Just a few swerves from the straight line, but once you stuff it with a pillow, I doubt anyone will notice."

"The corners were hard."

Mark smoothed the fabric on the counter. "It looks like you tried to round them." He glanced up at Sarah.

She shook her head.

"All you needed to do is stop in the corner—" Mark pointed to the fabric "—leave your needle in the fabric, lift the presser foot, and turn the fabric like this." Mark used his finger to demonstrate the turn. "Next time you come in to practice, I'll show you."

"I thought you didn't know how to sew." Sarah's eyes narrowed as she grinned.

"Just enough to demonstrate the machines I sell." Mark winked at Sarah and handed her the pillow top.

Sarah turned the panel right side out and finger pressed the edges. Intent on the task at hand, she cleared her throat. "I know we'll see each other before Sunday, but can we firm up the time for our date?"

The date! Pink painted Sarah's cheeks when she lifted a tentative gaze to Mark, waiting for his reply. He'd been so focused on Sarah's condition that he'd forgotten he'd asked her out. Was her diagnosis the reason her previous love dumped her? Anger prickled Mark's insides at the thought. Who'd do that? In an instant his mind answered his question. *A Sanders man.*

Mark's eyes met Sarah's. He should stop this now. Tell her that he was out of line, asking her out. Explain about his dad. His heart pounded at the thought of hurting her feelings, but better now than later. He drew in a deep, steadying breath. He had to break the date.

Anticipation sparkled in Sarah's dark eyes, melting Mark's resolve.

"Sure, what time works best for you?"

Sarah stuffed her pillow top into her denim tote bag. "Early afternoon?"

"I'll pick you up at one."

"Okay." Sarah looked around the counter. "If you have a pen, I'll write down my address."

Mark slid a pen and paper toward Sarah, even though he had her address on the class sign-up sheet.

Sarah wrote out the relevant information then pushed the paper and pen back to Mark. "All set, then." She pulled her car keys from her bag. "I'll see you tomorrow night."

Mark stepped around the counter. "Not so fast. I'll walk you to your car."

"My car is right there." Sarah pointed to her compact parked in the spot in front of the quilt shop door. She held her key fob and pressed a button.

"I know." Mark pulled the door open. His bell and Sarah's car horn clamored for attention. He held his palm up, indicating to Sarah to pass through the door.

"Thank you," Sarah said then stopped by the bumper of her car.

"You're welcome." Mark stepped off the curb, opened her car door, and waited for Sarah to slip into the seat. "Now you can say it."

"See you tomorrow night." Sarah giggled as she inserted the key into the ignition.

"Can't wait." Mark closed the car door and stepped back onto the curb. Before heading back into the store, he watched Sarah back out of the parking spot and turn into the street.

He lined up carts then walked through the store, straightening fabric bolts. He'd fully intended on breaking their date, but Sarah looked so happy and beautiful, he just couldn't bring himself to hurt her. *Besides, it appears that she's been hurt enough.*

And maybe, just maybe, his dating theory could do double duty for Sarah. He could give her self-confidence in moving on to a new relationship and insights on how to deal with everything that MS threw at her. In six short weeks, by the time the MS walk ended, she'd be taking better care of herself and ready to spread her wings to find her true love. And once again, his interim-man work would be done.

Chapter 5

The clock told Sarah that she was running behind on Saturday morning preparations. She grabbed her teakettle, stuck it under the faucet, and twisted the cold-water lever.

Managing the building, attending church committee meetings, and working on her quilt kept her too busy to have downtime. She'd slept late, hoping to relieve some of the fatigue that plagued her all week. She certainly didn't need her MS symptoms to act up on Sunday afternoon.

A thrill shivered through her as she thought of spending uninterrupted time alone with Mark. She couldn't wait. She hoped the weatherman's prediction proved accurate: a warm spring day in eastern South Dakota, God's reward for the frigid winter winds.

Mark's reaction the night she told him that she had MS puzzled her. His face drained of color, and panic flashed in his eyes. She never dreamed that her simple statement would bring a flood of memories of his mother's struggle. That had to have been what happened. Not that she had much practice or luck reading people, as her past could testify. The remainder of the night, although polite, he seemed distracted.

Yet Tuesday night, before and after class, he charmed her with playful teasing about his anticipation of their impending date. His text messages and e-mails throughout the week brightened her days. He seemed anxious to get to know her on a deeper level.

Happiness warmed her heart and brought a smile to her face. Like Job, she trusted God enough to take the bad with the good. She'd embraced her MS diagnosis, and now God rewarded her by bringing Mark into her life.

Sarah placed the filled teakettle on the stove at the same time a car pulled into her driveway. Her mother was an angel for not insisting Sarah drive to Brookings every Saturday morning. Wouldn't her mom be surprised to find out that Sarah had a date tomorrow? Sarah unlocked the back door and swung it open wide.

"Good morning."

"Well, you are chipper this fine April morning. You're almost beaming." Karla carried a bakery box and stepped through the door.

"Surprise!" Sarah's mother followed behind.

Sarah's heart fell, and the narrow-eyed glare she gave her mom as she passed by could not be described as beaming. Her mother stopped and placed her hand on Sarah's shoulder. She leaned in and pecked a kiss on Sarah's cheek. "Have an open mind, dear," she whispered.

How many times would Sarah have to tell her mother that she, Sarah, was the open-minded one? Karla practically had her in a nursing home by the age of forty.

The whistle of the teakettle broke the silence and called for Sarah's attention. She stepped around her mom. She deliberately kept her back to the two women as she filled the teapot, adding that and another cup to her serving tray while the tea brewed. How dare they gang up on her?

"I'll carry that." Karla voice startled Sarah. She nudged Sarah away from in front of the counter and lifted the wicker tray.

"I am capable of carrying a tray," Sarah mumbled. Her mother shot her a narrow-eyed stare as Sarah followed Karla to the table.

"*Tsk, tsk, tsk.*" Karla clicked her tongue as she set the tray on the table. "You don't have to do it all. Now sit."

Although the words sounded bossy, Karla's tone was light, so Sarah ignored the double meaning and slipped into a chair. Karla arranged the teapot and cups on the table as Sarah's mom served the cinnamon rolls.

"Thank you." Sarah smiled.

Karla carefully poured tea into their cups.

First Mark saw her safely into her car, and now she was being served. Sarah had to admit it felt nice.

"Hasn't the weather been beautiful?" Her mother smeared butter over her roll. "I've been watching the birds gather supplies for their nests."

"Yes." Karla's cup rattled against the saucer as she set it down. "It's helping my flower shoots get taller with each passing day. How's it affecting you?"

Again, Karla's tone held a friendly lilt, but the pointed look she aimed at Sarah emphasized the comment's double meaning. "I'm feeling fine, if that's what you're getting at. The temperatures aren't nearly warm enough to aggravate my MS. However, stress is a big trigger." Sarah kept her voice conversational and looked wide eyed at Karla as she delivered her double entendre response.

Karla's shoulders stiffened. She set her mouth and jutted out her chin.

"Well," Sarah's mom interjected, "that didn't take long."

Sarah tilted her head toward her mother. "Which one of you planned this little intervention?" This time she didn't hold back, her voice shaking with anger.

Her mother raised her hands in a stick-'em-up fashion. "I did. I just couldn't stand aside and see a long-term friendship dissolve over something as minor as a difference in opinion about a job."

"So you think that by ganging up on me, I'll cave and quit my job?" Not that the thought of resigning hadn't crossed her mind several times this week. The solitude of the building management job wore on her nerves. She missed her former job's hectic pace of delivering packages and having sporadic conversations with the customers on her route. She had way too much time to contemplate the grim future her disease would eventually bring. But she'd never admit that, especially to these two.

Her mother reached across the table for Sarah's hand. "We love you and we're concerned about your well-being. Plain and simple, you're doing too much."

"Yes, it's like you have something to prove. If you won't look out for yourself, then we, as people who care about you, have no choice but to do it for you." Karla reached for Sarah's other hand.

Sarah pulled her arms from the table and crossed them over her chest just like Mark's familiar gesture. Sarah grinned at the thought.

"What is so funny?" Karla snipped.

"Absolutely nothing. I just had a nice thought. Or is that against *your* rules now, too?"

"Really, Sarah." Her mother pursed her lips. "Of course we want you to be happy, but you need to listen to reason. You may be doing more harm than good to your body by keeping a busy schedule. You just said that stress triggered symptoms."

"And this—" Sarah waved her splayed fingers palms down in small circles "—isn't stress?" She paused to check her anger. "I used to enjoy getting together with both of you, but now I dread it. All we talk about is how I shouldn't do anything, yet I'm under a doctor's care and he's pleased with my progress."

"Touché." Her mom took a sip of her tea.

Karla exaggerated an eye roll. "I guess you made your point. No more badgering from me."

"Me either." Her mom cut a bit of her roll and stabbed it with her fork. "So then, tell us what's new."

"Funny you should ask." Sarah looked from her mom to Karla then slipped from her chair and rummaged through her purse. She returned to the table. "I'm taking part in the upcoming MS walk. Would either of you like to sponsor me?"

"Of course." Her mother reached for the form and pen. "Do you *have* to walk or can you just collect contributions?"

"Mom, I thought we were done with that conversation." Sarah sighed.

"It was just a question. But I am your mother and have a right to be concerned."

"I plan to walk the entire route. If I need to stop halfway I can, and if my MS flares up, I don't have to walk at all."

"Fair enough." Her mother marked the form then passed it to Karla.

Karla glanced at the form before laying it on the table. "How are you doing in that quilting class?" She didn't even try to hide her smirk.

"Well..." Sarah stood and retrieved her denim tote bag from the hall closet. "I'll let you two be the judge of that." She pulled out her three completed quilt blocks.

"I like the colors." Her mom picked up one and inspected it. She picked up the second one and knitted her brows.

Sarah began to laugh. "Yeah, you can say it. They don't quite match."

Karla reached over and grabbed them. "Are they even sewed the same?" She turned one at a different angle.

"No. The one you're holding I tried to sew on the sewing machine."

"But you don't know how to sew." Karla looked at the back of the block.

"Exactly. I thought all quilts were sewn by hand. Turns out that's not true."

Her mom snatched the quilt blocks back and turned them over. "These two look the best."

"They're the ones that I've sewn by hand. There are still mistakes but nothing like the one I tried on the machine. However—" she pulled the pillow top from the bag "—I didn't do bad sewing the pillow panel."

"Pillow? What does that have to do with a quilt?" Her mom passed the quilt blocks back to Karla and took the sham from Sarah.

"Nothing. I needed something to practice sewing on and that's what I chose."

"Are you renting a machine?" Karla lay the blocks on the table.

"No, Mark told me I could use the demonstrator machines at the quilt shop to learn to sew." Sarah gathered the quilt blocks and set them on top of the tote bag. "I've been stopping in about three nights a week to practice."

She caught the raised-eyebrow exchange between her mom and Karla. "What?"

"You practice sewing after a long day at work?" Her mom topped off their cups.

"Yes."

"How long do you stay and practice?" Karla crumpled her napkin then placed it on her plate before pushing it away from her.

Sarah knew better than to say until closing time. "Not that long."

"You go directly from work?" The terse tone and pursed lips were back.

"Yes." Sarah braced. Didn't they just promise to drop these lectures?

Karla gave a little snort. "I told you. She does too much. She isn't taking care of herself."

Tension thickened the air. Sarah watched her mother and Karla exchange another look as if they were talking to a five-year-old.

"I hope you're not skipping meals, because you need your stamina."

Was her mother serious? Of course she was. Authority dripped from her voice. Had the entire situation not been so maddening, Sarah might have laughed at the statement.

"Obviously, you don't really understand my condition." Sarah purposely infused her response with sarcasm. "It doesn't matter if you eat. Stamina's one of the first things to go with MS."

Sarah watched her mother's cheeks begin to flame with color, a telltale sign of anger. If they were going to treat her like a kindergartner, then she might as well play the part.

"Since you didn't answer the question, we can only assume that means you're skipping meals." Karla picked up the discussion and nodded toward Sarah's uneaten cinnamon roll.

Defiance surged through her, and her chest tightened. "I can't eat when I'm being badgered," she snapped back at Karla. "But to answer your question, Mother, I do eat. Sometimes I stop before I go to the quilt store, and sometimes Mark and I have dinner in the work…" Sarah stopped. She heard each thud of the dirge before her pulse beat out the rhythm. She'd just given them more ammunition. She should've kept Mark out of it.

"Sarah." Her mother's voice softened. "Now is not the time to get involved with a man."

"I already told her that. No man is going to want to be a caregiver."

"Karla, stop talking about me like I'm not sitting right beside you."

"I know you don't believe me, but you are setting yourself up to get hurt. Again."

Salty tears stung Sarah's eyes. She squeezed them shut, trying to will the tears away, but instead forced the warm moisture out onto her lashes. Did one bad mistake in her youth mean she shouldn't ever try love again?

Another surge of hurt leaked from the corners of her eyes. She sniffled. This relationship wasn't one sided like the last one. After all, Mark asked her out.

Sarah opened her eyes and reached for her cloth napkin. She dabbed at the moisture on her face, leaving mascara streaks on the eggshell linen. "This is different. Mark *is* interested in me."

Her mother's audible sigh increased the cloud of tension in the room. "Sarah, I hate to ask this but what are you basing his interest on? Helping you with purchases in his store?"

"Or by talking you into paying for quilting classes when you don't even know how to sew?" Karla patted the Job's Tears quilt block lying on the table. "That only shows his interest in profit, not in you."

The muscles in Sarah's shoulder grew taut. She rolled her right shoulder to alleviate the strain. *God, please don't let this flare the numbness in my right arm. I want to feel good for my date.*

"He's interested because he asked me out on a date." Sarah spoke through clenched teeth. She raised her shoulder and rested her ear on it. No relief.

"Have you been honest and told him that you have MS?" Her mother rose from her chair and stood behind Sarah. Her grip firm, she kneaded Sarah's muscles, helping to relax the tightness.

Sarah straightened then shook her right arm. God answered her prayers—no numbness. "Yes."

"What did he say?" The side of Karla's mouth curled up and she leaned forward, resting her chin in her hands. It was obvious to Sarah she was hoping for the worst.

"Nothing. I sort of blurted it out when I asked if I could join his team on the MS walk." Sarah leaned back in her chair as her mother continued to massage her neck and shoulders.

"Does he have MS?" Her mother stopped rubbing Sarah's shoulder and upper arm muscles.

"No." Sarah shook her head. "His mother did. The team walks and raises contributions as a memorial to her."

"Well, I guess he's used to dealing with someone with MS." Her mom patted Sarah's shoulders and slid back into her chair.

Finally her mother was seeing her point of view. Mark was used to someone with MS. He knew what to expect of the disease and how to handle it.

"When did you tell him you have MS? Before or after he asked you out?"

Karla just wouldn't let the subject die. Now maybe her mother would see what she'd been dealing with for months.

"After. Why?"

"I thought so." Karla smirked. "I doubt that he'd have asked you for a date had he known before that you were sick."

"You're wrong." Sarah looked to her mom for support but received a slight head shake instead.

"Sorry, honey, I think Karla's right. Had you disclosed your MS prior to him asking, that'd be different."

To give her mother credit, her face showed her remorse in her belief, but that didn't stop Sarah's heart from crumbling like a cinnamon roll, the bits of which now littered her empty plates.

"But he didn't cancel after he found out." Sarah whispered her response as she remembered Mark's strange reaction. Was he wondering how he could retract his offer of a date instead of thinking about his mom? That couldn't be, because he'd been texting her all week, telling her how much he was looking forward to Sunday afternoon.

Sarah mustered all her bravado. She cleared her throat and sat up straighter. "He didn't cancel after he found out." This time she said the words with certainty. "As a matter of fact, he sent me a text yesterday, telling me how much he's looking forward to it."

"Okay, so he's not a jerk. He'll go through with this date. Then what? Are you really going to want to continue with quilting class or be on his walking team when he doesn't want to see you on a personal level anymore?"

Karla reached for Sarah's hand, but Sarah yanked it away and rested it in her lap. How could she make them understand that she wanted to live, no, *needed* to live as normal a life as possible? She looked down at her Job's Tears quilt blocks. Like Job, she'd cried out in anger to God after her diagnosis, but since she'd found the quilt shop and Mark, her anger concerning her MS disappeared.

She couldn't let them rob her of the good in her life. In time she'd prove them wrong. Mark wasn't the shallow type, she could tell. Sarah drew a deep breath, but before she could answer, her cell phone rang.

"Excuse me." Sarah jumped from her seat. Happiness inflated her chest as "You've Got a Friend," the tune she'd assigned to Mark, cut through the tense silence in the room. Sarah ran for her purse, glad for the distraction from the conversation.

"Hello, Mark." Joy softened Sarah's voice as she flashed a triumphant smile toward the table.

"Hi, Sarah."

The edge in Mark's voice told her bad news would follow.

"I'm sorry to do this on such short notice, but I have to break our date."

Chapter 6

After church Sarah changed into her gray yoga pants and matching gray-and-pink T-shirt and settled on the couch to work on her Job's Tears quilt blocks. She spread the contents from her tote bag onto the adjoining cushion for easy access. Holding a block, she maneuvered the seam ripper through the machine stitching on the seams, cutting the small stitches and being careful not to tear the fabric. The one thing her mom and Karla had been right about yesterday was that the hand-sewn blocks looked much better.

They weren't right about Mark, though. He had a good reason for canceling their date this afternoon. One of his two part-time clerks quit without prior notice. He had to cover her shift. After his call, Sarah had found it hard to swallow her disappointment. She'd managed to keep her voice light and her answers generic until her mom and Karla said their good-byes.

The last thing she needed to hear from Karla yesterday was "I told you so." Her friend had planted enough doubts that, at first, Sarah worried that Mark was trying to get out of their date. But the more she thought about it, the more she realized her concern was unfounded. She dropped by the store often enough and spent enough time with Mark that if he were lying, she was fairly confident she'd pick up on it. Besides, he'd insisted that they reschedule as soon as he could get a new work schedule in place.

Sarah smoothed out the loose pieces of fabric before pinning the edge together. She threaded her needle then inserted it into the cloth. Her hand sewing showed improvement despite some faint numbness in her upper arm.

The rhythmic movement caused her mind to wander to the verse from Ecclesiastes the lector read in church this morning. *"When times are good, be happy; but when times are bad, consider this: God has made the one as well as the other. Therefore, no one can discover anything about their future."*

She wished her mother and Karla had attended this morning's service at Sarah's small country church. Then they'd see the goal she was striving for in her life—acceptance that God was in control. Right now she was happy, unlike a few months ago. Her life seemed full of hope again since meeting Mark, starting a new job, and finding a hobby. Sarah didn't know if Mark was a permanent fixture in her future. She hoped and prayed he was, but only God knew for certain.

Engrossed in her sewing, she jumped when the doorbell rang.

"Ouch!" Sarah dropped her sewing. As she walked

to the front door, she rubbed the finger she'd poked with the needle. She hoped this wasn't a surprise visit from Karla. She wasn't up to another conversation like yesterday's.

She peeked out the window and saw a florist delivery van parked behind her car. Sarah opened the door.

"Are you Sarah Buckley?"

"Yes."

"These are for you." The teenage delivery boy shoved a vase of cut flowers toward her then turned. "Have a great day," he called over his shoulder.

Sarah balanced the heavy glass vase against her side as she closed her door. The sweet scent of irises delighted her nose. She set the large vase on the end table and admired the spring bouquet of daisies, irises, tulips, and crocuses. Slipping the card from the plastic holder, she dipped her nose into the arrangement and inhaled the flowers' bouquet. Was this her mom's or Karla's way of saying, "I'm sorry"?

Sarah opened the envelope and read the card.

I hope these flowers brighten your day. Sorry I had to break our date. See you tomorrow night, Mark.

Happiness fluttered through Sarah, forcing out a giggle. She read the card again and savored the joyous feeling. She knew she was right about Mark. A man who wasn't interested would never send a girl flowers.

She removed an African violet from the stand in front of the picture window and set the plant on the floor. She placed the flowers on the mosaic-topped stand that was right in her line of vision from the sofa where she planned to be the remainder of the afternoon, sewing quilt blocks.

Sarah lifted her cell phone from the end table and sat down cross-legged on the couch. She nervously fingered a throw pillow with one hand as she hit the programmed number in her cell phone. She smiled as the connection began to ring. She definitely hoped God included Mark in her future.

The tissue paper Sarah wrapped around her flowers to protect them in the car worked. Not one flower petal was broken or missing. As she stood back and admired the bouquet sitting on the corner of her desk, she shivered with giddiness.

"Hoo-wee, someone's been a good girl." Ashley strode up behind her then whistled. "That's one beautiful bouquet."

"You won't get an argument from me." Sarah giggled.

"Tell Mark he did good."

"How did you know he sent them? I haven't shown you the card yet."

"Sarah, where Mark's concerned you haven't a poker face."

Sarah shrugged and giggled again. She reveled in the lighter-than-air feeling.

"Judging by the flowers, I can tell he's just as smitten with you as you are with him." Ashley squeezed Sarah's shoulders.

Surprised by the happy tears that welled in her eyes, Sarah swiped away the moisture with the back of her knuckle. It felt so good to have someone share her happiness about her relationship.

"Let's get some coffee, and you can tell me all about your date."

Ashley headed for the adjoining room. Sarah grabbed her cup and inhaled deeply as she passed her flowers. The spring fragrance tickled her senses. Mark's gesture delighted her heart.

Sarah held her cup steady while Ashley poured.

"So spill it." Ashley set the carafe on the warming element.

Ashley pulled a face when she saw Sarah pretending to spill her coffee. "I didn't mean that and you know it. Tell me about your date."

Sarah sipped her coffee. "There's nothing to tell."

"What?" Ashley frowned and looked out toward the flowers.

"One of Mark's employees quit with no notice. He had to cover the shift. The bouquet is part of his apology for canceling our date, and he promised to reschedule, so…" Sarah zigzagged her fingers over the textured surface of her gold-toned earring. "I'm sure he really does want to date me."

"What is that supposed to mean?" Ashley's frown deepened. "Of course he wants to date you—he asked you out."

It took a minute for Sarah to realize exactly what she said. She waved her hand in the air. "Well, my mom and friend seem to think now that Mark knows I have—" She stopped. She'd never told Ashley that she, Sarah, had MS.

She cleared her throat. "Ashley, I have multiple sclerosis. The people closest to me seem to think now that Mark knows my medical condition, he won't want to date me."

"Really? Why would that make a difference? Don't they want you to be happy? I don't understand that line of thinking at all." Ashley slipped down into a chair by the break-room table. Her nostrils flared and, as she frowned, deeper creases lined her forehead. She seemed to have skipped right past Sarah's illness to anger in defending Sarah's rights.

Sarah furrowed her brow. "You think it wouldn't make a difference to a man if a woman were sick. If he wanted to date her, he would."

"Absolutely. Don't they trust your judgment in men?"

They didn't, and Sarah couldn't blame them. They'd helped her pick up the pieces once. Sarah swallowed hard in an attempt to clear her throat of the bitter pill of past mistakes as she responded to Ashley's question with a slight shake of the head.

"Besides, you look healthy. What does having MS mean, exactly?" Ashley gave Sarah a once-over before taking a drink of her coffee.

"Right now, it means that I lose muscle control in my right arm from time to time. Lots of things can bring on an attack, like the weather, stress, or fatigue. When that happens, I go get a steroid shot and the symptoms usually clear right up."

"Here's to modern medicine and a hope for a cure." Ashley held her travel mug up.

Sarah lightly tapped it with her coffee mug in agreement with the toast. "Speaking of that, I'm taking part in the MS walk. I have a sign-up sheet at my desk if you'd like to sponsor me."

"Sure."

Ashley followed Sarah into the office area. As Ashley wrote down her pledge, the office door opened.

Sarah looked up, ready to give her pat "good morning" or "may I help you." Her heart fluttered. "Mark! What are you doing here?"

Dressed in blue jeans and the green polo shirt that emphasized the emerald flecks in his eyes, Mark held up a box of doughnuts. "Peace offering."

After polite introductions and small talk, Sarah's tenant excused herself.

"I won't get you into trouble just stopping by, will I?" Mark hadn't realized how much he'd looked forward to his date with Sarah until she'd called to thank him for the flowers.

Sarah shrugged. "My bosses are located in the downtown office, and I'm supposed to get breaks, but I usually work through them. Sometimes my lunch, too, so I think I can take a short break now."

Mark wrinkled his brow. Sarah should take her breaks if for no other reason than to ward away the fatigue that accompanied MS.

She started across the room and waved for Mark to follow along.

He hadn't expected such a formal office. The plush carpet and bulky cherrywood desk screamed dignified. No wonder Sarah's attire was always accessorized and polished.

Today was no different. A lavender linen jacket topped her floral-print dress with a formfitting skirt. The back slit in the skirt might have been designed for easier movement, but it showcased Sarah's slender, shapely calves. Her spike-heeled sandals, a shade darker than the jacket, added at least three inches to her height.

"Are you coming?" Sarah peeked around the door.

Mark entered the long room. A stark contrast to Sarah's office area, the office machine room that appeared to double as a break room was decorated in white-and-gray run-of-the-mill counters and clapboard cupboards. He set the doughnuts on the white plastic-topped folding table.

"You look lovely today. You do justice to every color you wear." Mark took the cup of steaming liquid she offered, savoring the flush that deepened the color of Sarah's cheeks.

"Thank you." Sarah's black eyes glistened. "Why did you call the doughnuts a peace offering? I'm not angry with you."

Mark chuckled. "For my conscience. I really hated standing you up yesterday."

"Well, many thanks to you and your conscience for this treat." Sarah removed a doughnut from the box and held it up. "And for your surprise visit. You've made my day."

"Likewise." Mark smiled. Should he tell her she'd been making his day every time she stopped into his store?

"I hope you didn't go out of your way."

"Actually, I didn't. I live in the condos not far from here." Mark pointed to the southeast.

"In the new development?" Sarah nibbled at her glazed doughnut.

Mark nodded his head. "You sound surprised." Only two-thirds of his doughnut was left after his first bite.

"I guess I assumed because you were a lifelong resident of Sioux Falls that you'd live in a more established neighborhood."

"We did, but after Mom passed away I downsized.

Unlike Caroline's fiancé, Rodney, I dislike yard work and snow removal especially after a long day of work, so I sold Grandma's house and bought a condo."

"Makes sense. I don't enjoy those activities, either. I rent my Kiwanis Avenue duplex. The owner and his wife live in the other side. He is very particular about his lawn, so he takes care of those things for me."

Good, because you shouldn't be doing that kind of work anyway. Mark broke a sugar-coated doughnut in two and dunked one end into his coffee.

"Thank you again for the treat." Sarah wiped icing from her fingers.

"I should thank you for indulging me. I thought it'd be nice to have friendly company before I start a long day." Mark popped the last of his doughnut into his mouth.

"Another one?" Sarah's dark eyes clouded. "If you want to talk about what happened and why your clerk quit, I don't mind."

Was she a mind reader? As soon as it had happened, he'd almost called Sarah to talk. It was the first time he'd wanted to talk to someone other than his mom when he had a problem. He'd actually picked up the phone then reconsidered.

He wiped his mouth and hands on his napkin. "Rachel's daughter ran into some trouble with the law, so she's moving her grandchildren to her house."

"Sounds like Rachel's family needs our prayers." Sarah twisted her earring as she shook her head.

"I'd say so. It's a sad situation, but Rachel's doing the right thing for the children. She hated to quit with no notice, but given the circumstances she just didn't feel like she could leave them with a sitter while she worked for two weeks."

"So now you're shorthanded."

"Yes. I'm covering her shifts this week until Terri and I can work out a schedule. I'm heading in to work early so I can get some special orders placed before it's time to open." Mark sighed. "Compared to what Rachel's going through, a few long workdays is nothing, but…"

"You're not looking forward to it." Sarah's eyes conveyed sympathy.

"As much as I like running the quilt shop, I'm not looking forward to several eleven-hour days."

"It does get tiring. I delivered for UPS for twenty years and pulled long shifts during holiday times." Sarah's expression changed to wistful.

"You had to change jobs because of your MS?"

"Yes, the heavy lifting and summer heat made my symptoms flare, so I opted for a climate-controlled job." She held her hands up, but sadness showed on her face.

"I can tell you miss your old job."

"I miss being busy and chatting with a variety of people each day. It's hit or miss most days here on both accounts. Although I'll find out later today if a large company decided to lease the third floor. If they do I'll be overseeing the remodeling project." Sarah's face brightened.

Mark frowned. He knew how stressful it could be working with contractors, not to mention lessees. She'd be right in the middle of trying to please everyone. Not a good position for an MS patient to be in. "That sounds like a lot of work."

"I prefer to think of it as a challenge." Sarah rubbed her palms together.

Mark smiled at her enthusiasm but made a mental note to make sure she took care of herself if the remodel deal went through. "Speaking of challenges, I have my own to handle today. I'd better head to the store and place those orders before it's time to open." Mark stood. "And I'm sure I stayed longer than I should have."

Sarah waved his comment off. "Don't worry about it. I'll eat my lunch at my desk. And as you can tell, the phone hasn't rung once since you arrived." She put their coffee cups into the kitchen sink and followed Mark into her office area.

Mark slowed his steps to stretch their last moments together. He reached for her hand and cupped it the way he had the night he demonstrated the sewing machine. He felt the familiar curves where the back of her hand met her knuckles, her short, plump fingers, the feathery softness of her skin.

He stopped by the door and searched her face. The soft curve at the corner of her lips beckoned to him. He licked his lips in an attempt to stop the nervous quiver that urged him to kiss Sarah. It didn't work. He leaned toward her. When their eyes met, hers widened.

He'd never wanted to kiss any woman more than at this moment. He'd never wanted to hold any woman close and feel her warmth like he wanted to do with Sarah. He never wanted protect any woman like he wanted to protect Sarah.

Her hand trembled in his, reminding him that their surroundings weren't the appropriate place for a first kiss. He squeezed her hand before lifting it to his lips and pressing a kiss in her palm, never breaking eye contact. He folded her fingers over the spot he kissed.

"Hold on to this for me." He knew his kiss would be safe with Sarah.

"You are the prettiest sandwich-delivery person I've ever seen." Mark pulled a foot-long sub from a plastic bag.

Sarah giggled. Since Mark kissed her palm she'd been floating in a bubble of happiness.

"Aren't you eating?" Mark lifted the bag and shook out the napkins. "I can share."

"It's all yours. I ate mine on the drive over." Sarah turned on the demonstrator machine. "I need all the time I can get to try and sew a quilt block on the machine before the class starts. I ended up ripping the last one apart and sewing it by hand."

Mark brought his sandwich and drink to the middle of the worktable as Sarah spread out her supplies. "Will it bother you if I sit here and watch?"

"No, but it may bother you to watch a woman who has absolutely no idea how to sew since you're not used to that," Sarah teased Mark.

He gave her a weary smile. "It won't bother me. You're so thoughtful to bring me dinner."

"I told you I know what it's like to work long hours. Little things matter." Besides, she wanted to touch his heart the way he melted hers with the surprise visit to her office.

"I saw the Help Wanted sign in the window. Has anyone applied?" Sarah lined up two pieces of contrasting fabric then tucked them under the presser foot.

"Not yet. I did have a lady inquire, thinking that

her daughter may be interested in it. However, Terri's daughter is home from college in a week. She has a summer internship lined up, but that doesn't start until the first of June, so Terri's going to see if she'd like to fill the open position to earn some extra money." Mark raised the straw to his mouth.

The simple gesture warmed Sarah's palm where he'd placed his sweet kiss. "That sounds like the perfect solution. Then you can take your time finding the right person for the position."

Mark nodded as he chewed a bite of sandwich.

The machine whirred as Sarah guided her fabric toward the needle. "Darn."

"What?" Mark looked over.

"My fabric keeps slipping." Sarah lifted the presser foot and pulled the pieces free.

"You need to pin it together." Mark wiped his hands on his napkin.

"Then how will I sew it? Won't pins break the needle?"

Mark shook his head as he stood. Sarah forgot her quilt project as she watched him walk around the table and stop beside her. His navy-striped polo shirtsleeves stretched tight across his biceps. The sharp crease in his navy trousers, a shade lighter from consistent pressing, led down to athletic shoes.

"I knew I'd be on my feet all day." He lifted one foot. "I wanted to be comfortable in case the Tuesday night special works. My timing wasn't good concerning the start of that, but…"

"I was just thinking what a smart man you were, wearing practical shoes on a long day." Sarah thought she saw the circumference of Mark's chest increase a little as his instant smile pushed all the weariness from his features.

"You—" Mark tapped the end of her nose with his forefinger "—are just what I needed today."

His intense stare made Sarah hold her breath. Would he kiss her?

Mark leaned toward her, closing the gap between them. The emotion conveyed in his hazel eyes caused a rapid pattering of her heart. His warm breath tickled her cheek. Sarah leaned forward and tilted her chin, ready to receive his kiss.

A light rap on the workroom door broke their eye contact. "Sorry to interrupt your dinner, but it's time for me to leave." Terri threw her boss an apologetic look.

Sarah caught the slight tremble of Mark's hand as he glanced at his watch. Was attraction surging through him, too? Numbing his thoughts and putting his senses on high alert?

"Go ahead and leave." Mark's baritone held a bass edge. He cleared his throat. "I'll go out to the sales floor as soon as I show Sarah a sewing method."

"Thanks. I'll see you tomorrow at noon." Terri gave them a wiggle-finger wave as she left through the back door.

"Let's start with two new pieces of your pattern." Mark held out a steady hand.

Sarah lifted two pieces of her quilt block, hoping Mark didn't see her own hand shake from her palpitating heart, and laid them in Mark's outstretched palm. How had he gained control in such a short time?

Mark lined up the raw edges of Sarah's quilt blocks. "Slide your straight pins over to me." He pinched several pins out of her plastic pin container and scattered them on the table. "This is what you need to do." He poked each of the pins into cloth so that the sharp end was even with the raw edge of the fabric. He handed it back to Sarah.

She studied the pins lined up a few inches apart. "Do I take the pins out as I sew?"

"You could, but I think you'd have better luck leaving them in until your seam was finished. Don't worry. The machine will stitch right over the pins. Try it."

Sarah lined the fabric up with the seam-measurement marker on the sewing machine. She lowered the presser foot and slowly pushed down on the foot feed. Concentrating on her sewing, Sarah began to regain control of her emotions. After a few minutes, she was finished. "That worked so much better!"

Mark's eyes crinkled from his wide smile. "Have fun practicing." He scooped his garbage up from the table and headed toward the door.

"Are you sure you don't know how to sew?" Sarah started pulling pins out of the material.

"Only enough to demonstrate the machines I sell." Mark winked then walked out the door.

Although the edges weren't even, Sarah had one block sewed by the time Caroline and her classmates started arriving. She wasn't sure if it was faster to sew by hand or the machine. Both took arm control. Yet MS tingled her arm as if it were asleep—more times than she cared to admit by this time of the day.

Once everyone was seated, Caroline began the class. "I just want everyone to work on their projects tonight. I'll walk through and check your progress or answer any questions that might have come up as you worked on your projects last week." She held up a table runner.

"I finished this during the week. I'll pass it around so you can see how the blocks look when they're finished and sewn together."

Caroline handed the table runner to Sarah, who ran her fingers over the Job's Tears blocks. Caroline had sewn the quilt's pattern pieces crisp and even, creating distinct angles that added to the beauty of the block. Sarah's heart sank a little. Even her hand-sewn blocks were jagged in spots, giving her block a choppy look. Karla was probably right—Sarah was wasting her time.

"While you're looking at the table runner, don't use it as a measure for your project. I've been sewing and quilting since I was teenager."

Sarah slowly lifted her eyes to Caroline.

"Your wistful expression gave you away. The very first quilt I ever made was four-by-four-inch blocks, in pink and orange, sewn in rows. Some had wide seams and some had narrow seams. At ten, I wanted to do whatever my mom did, so while she made a double-wedding-ring quilt for my grandparents' fortieth wedding anniversary, I stitched a psychedelic twin-sized quilt for my bed, which brings me to something I'd like to discuss tonight."

After examining the front and back of Caroline's table runner, Sarah passed it to one of the elderly ladies then resumed pinning more pieces together as the other machines' purrs mocked her lack of abilities. Yet the last block she sewed was her best work so far.

Caroline examined everyone's stacks of blocks and returned to the front of the room. She pulled a chair to the center. "I'm sorry I didn't bring my hippie quilt, as my grandmother donned it."

"You still have it?" the teenage girl asked.

"Yes, I do." Caroline laughed. "It's a little worse for wear but still serves its purpose. That brings me to what I want to talk about tonight. Every quilt has a story. You just heard the story of my first quilt. I made it because I wanted to be like my mother. Tonight, I'd like you to share with the class why you wanted to make a quilt so we'll all know your quilt's story."

Caroline smiled wide. Her laugh lines crinkled, emphasizing the love of her work. "Who wants to go first?"

Sarah's machine whirred as she tried to keep her fabric pieces lined up with the measurement guide. Between no sewing experience and a numbness interfering with her arm's control, she had to stop occasionally to realign the material. This required too much concentration for her to talk about her reason for enrolling in the quilting class. Plus, did she really want to disclose the number one reason she was here? She wasn't ashamed of her multiple sclerosis, but was it everyone's business? Sarah continued to try to get a fluid motion to her sewing.

After considerable silence, the elderly gentleman said, "I'll go first since I'm probably the least likely person to enroll in a quilting class. My granddaughter, Brystol, and I enrolled in the quilting class because our family voted last Christmas that this year's gifts would be homemade, so I'm making my wife a table runner for Christmas. I'm sure she thinks she'll get something made from wood since woodworking's my hobby."

"Won't she be surprised!" the second elderly lady interjected.

Sarah stopped sewing and turned to look at the gentleman. His face beamed with apparent love for his wife.

"I think so." The man winked at his granddaughter.

"And you sew so well, too. She will love it." The lady nodded her assurance to him.

"Grandpa ran a car upholstery business for years so he knows how to sew." Brystol smiled at her grandfather.

"So, does that mean you're making a family member a Christmas gift, too?" Caroline looked at the young girl.

Brystol stopped sewing. "Yes, for my older sister." She shrugged before refocusing on her work.

"I'm Mary and I'll go next." The chatty lady smoothed a finished quilt block with her fingers.

Sarah took a deep breath. She had sewn together only half a block in the time it took Mary to finish one. She continued to stitch while she listened.

"I'm selling my house and downsizing to a smaller apartment, so I decided to give myself a housewarming gift of a wall quilt."

Sarah cut the thread, releasing her cloth from the machine. She noticed a shade of sadness in the woman's expression. "What a wonderful way to celebrate a positive change in your life." Almost the same reason Sarah had enrolled in the class.

Mary brightened. "Thank you, dear."

"My table runner will be donated to my church bazaar," Mary's friend piped up.

"Sarah, you're up." Caroline shot her a sly smile.

What was that all about? Sarah left her pieces half-sewn in the machine and began to pin others together while she spoke. "About eighteen months ago, I was diagnosed with MS. I had to make some changes to my life, which ended up giving me a lot of free time."

Sarah's voice cracked and the last few words came out in a whisper.

Sudden emotion welled up in Sarah as she visualized those first few months of bitterness. She cleared her throat, hoping the rush of feelings didn't shake her voice again. What was wrong with her? She'd moved forward months ago. "So I decided I needed a hobby to fill up my time. I thought I'd better do it right away because who knows how long I'll be able to do intricate movements." The immediate flush of embarrassment burned her cheeks. Where had that come from? It might be true, but that was never a conscious reason she enrolled in the class.

"Grandpa, our quilt stories are kind of lame compared to everyone else's."

"No, they're not," Caroline said. "Because they're all made with love for a special reason—be it happiness, service, or healing. Recently a quilt not only brought me healing but happiness. As I restored a Lily of the Field quilt, I relearned the lesson of the Bible verse, Matthew 6:28–34, that the block was named for and remembered I need to trust God with my life. In addition, I fell in love with the quilt's owner."

"What a wonderful story about your quilt," Sarah said, remembering the number one reason for her enrolling in this class. Mark.

"Actually, that is all it is. A story about a quilt, although Rodney and I tried to find out the *real* story behind the quilt, the reason it was made, but we weren't successful."

Caroline stood and began to walk around her students. "I'd just like you all to remember to never underestimate the power of a quilt."

When Caroline patted her shoulder, Sarah jumped. Her knee-jerk reaction caused her to stop guiding her fabric but not lift her foot off the foot feed. As the needle buzzed up and down, the piece of fabric turned sideways. Sarah frowned and looked up at Caroline. Had she made an error while sewing?

Caroline's eyes met Sarah's. Her mouth curved in slyness that could match the Grinch's. "Healing and happiness. Quilts have a wonderful way of bringing people together."

Chapter 7

An electrician cracked Sarah's office door and stuck his head in. "Miss, the other contractor is tied up and won't make it out here until around six."

Sarah sagged in her chair. It was the third time this week. She rubbed the bicep of her right arm, knowing that it wouldn't relieve the symptoms. Six really meant seven, or not at all. On Wednesday night, she'd waited for a carpet person to come and measure the room. At seven, he'd finally called and canceled.

At least today she was smart enough to bring along her quilt blocks and a can of soup. She didn't know if it was acceptable or not to work on her project in the office, but she had to have something to do.

Sarah shook out the sewing supplies from her tote onto her desk then dropped her bag to the floor. For the millionth time, she mulled over what Caroline had said in class. Sarah had ripped the sentence apart and sewn it together so many ways, but the end result always seemed the same—Caroline saw through her where Mark was concerned. Maybe Mark mentioned something to Caroline?

Tired from the long working hours of the last three days, Sarah wished she could rest her head on her desk while she waited, but that would be unprofessional. Yet she knew a quick nap would do her a world of good since her MS had deadened her right biceps just after noon.

As Sarah struggled to thread her needle, she reminded herself that, like Job, she must take the bad—in this case long hours and the effects from MS—from the Lord, as well as the good.

At least the construction project filled her working hours and then some. The last two days, she'd played intermediary between the building managers, the construction people, and the new tenants. It was impossible to keep everyone happy, but she was trying.

Sarah wiggled her fingers, attempting to remove the frozen feeling from her right arm. After several attempts she managed to push the thread through the small needle eye. Her hand sewing would be difficult tonight. She pushed the needle into the fabric, trying to use the fingers of her left hand to guide the implement back up and into the material.

"Ouch!" Having poked herself with the needle, Sarah rubbed the tip of her middle finger with her thumb. She glanced at the clock. She really wanted to stop at the quilt shop tonight to practice sewing and see Mark. She'd almost called him earlier to see if she could bring him something for dinner. However, because of her arm tingling, she doubted she could guide the fabric through the machine any better than she could hand sew.

Sarah tried another way to control the needle, but it was no use. She could barely feel it between her fingers, let alone guide it into her fabric.

Ashley breezed in from the hallway. "What are you still doing here?"

"Waiting on a construction person so they can give me a bid for the remodel." Sarah began to gather her quilting supplies with her left hand.

"You look beat."

"I am. Fatigue is a major symptom with MS." Sarah unsuccessfully tried to put fabric in her tote bag.

"What's wrong?" Ashley dropped her briefcase and purse to the floor and stepped closer to Sarah.

"It's just my MS. It affects my right arm."

Ashley frowned as she snatched Sarah's bag from the floor and held it open. "You need to go home."

"I can't. The new client wants the bid first thing in the morning." Sarah sighed and dropped her sewing supplies into the tote. If she could just lie down for a few minutes, she'd feel much better.

"Do you have any medicine or anything to take?" Ashley put Sarah's tote on the floor beside her own.

"I do, but I'd rather wait until I get home." Sarah glanced up at the wall clock and wished the contractor would hurry.

"Understandable. Should you be driving?"

Sarah heard the genuine concern in Ashley's voice, unlike the tone Karla used with Sarah. "I'll be fine." She forced happiness into her voice and smiled at Ashley. Sarah would be fine if she just rested a few minutes while she waited for the contractor to arrive.

"I don't know about that. Listen, I don't have any plans for tonight. I can wait around and drive you home." Ashley dropped into the reception area's guest chair.

The contractor stuck his head in the door once again. "They're here. I'll take them up so they can get started."

"I'll be right there." Thank goodness they came at the time they said they would. "Ashley, thank you for your offer, but I don't want to impose. Go home. I'll be fine." Sarah stood, but as soon as she put weight on her legs, the sensation in her right leg felt like tiny pins poking her muscles. She stamped her foot, trying to wake it up. "Great. My leg fell asleep."

She leaned against the desk and wiggled her ankle. No relief. Dread pulled at her heart. Maybe she'd just sat wrong, blocking the flow of blood to her leg. She stamped her foot again. Some improvement but a niggling sensation remained.

"Do you need some help?" Ashley stood.

Sarah took a tentative step. Better. "No, I'm fine, but maybe I shouldn't drive since I'm so tired. This shouldn't take long."

"No problem. Like I said before, I don't have plans."

Still half asleep, Sarah glanced at her digital alarm clock. When her mind registered the time, she sat straight up in bed. Her mother would arrive for their Saturday morning visit in few minutes.

Sarah flexed her right arm. It was amazing what a good night's sleep would do to lessen the numbness. Tentatively, she stepped out of bed. Sarah smiled, relieved that her leg felt normal. She must have just sat in the same position too long yesterday.

Sarah padded to the kitchen to start a pot of tea, smiling all the way. Today was the day. Anticipation shivered through her as she considered outfits for her date with Mark.

Just as she started to add water to the teakettle, the doorknob rattled.

"Just a minute, Mom." Sarah put the kettle in the sink before heading to the door. Unlocking the door with one hand, she twisted the knob with the other. Before she swung the door open, she drew a deep breath in case another surprise visit from Karla awaited her. Even that wouldn't dampen her spirits today.

"Good morning." She returned her mother's bright smile and sighed with relief that her mom was traveling alone this Saturday.

Her mother's smile faded as she gave her daughter the once-over. "Are you all right?"

Her mother's appraisal of Sarah's appearance as she entered the kitchen annoyed Sarah. So she was still in her pajamas and slippers at nine thirty in the morning. "I've been putting in long hours at work this week, so I slept in."

"Sarah, I'm telling you that you are taking on too much." Her mother pursed her lips before setting the bakery bag on the table. "I told your father that he needs to have a talk with you."

"What did Dad say to that?" Sarah removed two mugs and luncheon plates from the cupboard.

"He said you always sound fine and *happy* on the phone and that you were a big girl and could take care of yourself." Her mother took the mugs, filled them with water, and placed them in the microwave.

"Good, because he's right." Sarah shot her mother a

grin as she placed the cinnamon rolls on the plates and grabbed some napkins.

"I don't think so." Her mother pulled the paper covering from two tea bags. When the microwave timer went off, Sarah headed into the living room.

Her mother followed carrying the steaming mugs with a steady hand. She carefully set a mug on each end table.

Sarah waited for her mom to sit down then handed her a plate and napkin.

Her mother slipped off her sandals before tucking one leg under the other. Sarah joined her on the couch.

Sitting cross-legged, she faced her mother. Balancing her plate on her legs, she broke off a piece of her roll. The spicy burst of cinnamon followed by the sweet creaminess of frosting brought out a hum of appreciation from Sarah.

"Thank you for always bringing my favorite." Sarah smiled at her mother.

"You're welcome." Her mother cocked her head and studied Sarah. "Actually, your father may be right. Perhaps Karla has planted seeds of doubt in me. I don't think the sun will shine brighter today than the twinkle in your eyes. You must really love your job."

Happiness erupted in Sarah's heart. Her job had little to do with her beaming joy. That could only be attributed to Mark and the appreciation that flamed in his eyes when he looked at her. The internal quiver inspired by his touch. The zap of electric current that, days later, still tingled her palm where he'd kissed her. Sarah swallowed her bite of roll and drew a deep breath. She hoped her mother would share her excitement. "It's not my job. Today's my first official date with Mark."

The dropped gaze and pursed lips told Sarah that her mother didn't share her enthusiasm.

"Why can't you be happy for me?" Sarah hated the pleading sound of her voice.

"I don't want to see you get hurt again." Her mother placed her plate with the half-eaten roll on the floor beside the sofa. "I know that you don't think so, but you are vulnerable. I don't want someone taking advantage of you."

"Tell me, Mom, how is Mark taking advantage of me? He's never been anything but a gentleman."

"For one thing, you're not thinking clearly. You haven't been for months now. I'm sure he can sense that. People aren't always what they seem. You know that from experience." Her mother's raised eyebrows emphasized her point.

Sarah couldn't argue with that. But would that one mistake in love haunt her for the rest of her life? "This relationship is entirely different. I'm an entirely different person. I *know* that Mark's interest is genuine."

"Really? You are sure that he's not a married man?"

Now they could both see the elephant in the room. "Yes."

"Absolutely?"

"Why are you so against this relationship? I've dated several men since then, and you've never discouraged me. Is it because of my MS diagnosis?"

"No." Her mother lifted the plate from Sarah's legs then placed it on the floor atop her own. She slid closer to Sarah and grasped her hands. She searched her daughter's face before meeting her eyes.

"I am not against the relationship because of the MS. I believe that you can lead a very active life with your disease, but you are going to have to make adjustments. I never disapproved of your other relationships because I could tell that you weren't that serious about those men."

"How can you say that?"

"Because, Sarah, you have a certain look when you're falling in love. I saw it when you were in your twenties when you mistook signs from a professional acquaintance. I see the same look now."

Was she falling in love with Mark? The thought sparked a surge of happiness in her heart, chasing out her annoyance with her mother. "So, your daughter's being in love is a bad thing?" She'd admit she learned a hard lesson in her twenties, one she didn't plan to repeat. She pulled her hands free of her mother's grasp and rubbed her palm in the spot that had been branded by Mark's soft lips.

Her mother sighed. "See, it's there again. You're going into this relationship blindly. Are you going to be able to handle it if your heart gets broken? The last time it took you several years to bounce back. Now, with your medical condition, a depressive state like that could be, well, detrimental. The experience left you wary, but I just feel you've let that guard down with this man."

That was true. She'd allowed herself to trust Mark, ever since seeing his warm smile that first time she entered his store. The more she got to know him, the surer she was that his values were solid and his actions sincere. "Mark is different."

"We'll see." Her mother stood and paced to the window.

You will see. Mark is different. Just one more thing she had to prove to the world.

* * *

Mark pulled into Sarah's driveway about twenty minutes earlier than he was supposed to be there. If he hadn't driven around the neighborhood three times, he'd be thirty minutes early.

He slipped from his four-wheel-drive pickup. Sticking his hands in the front pockets of his khaki cargo shorts, he surveyed her home. The tan-sided duplex shared a driveway but provided privacy by having the double garages as the connecting point.

Mark didn't have to look at the house number to tell which side was Sarah's. A large wreath comprised of various pastel-colored flowers with a welcome sign in the center hung beside the door. Judging by her clothing choices, Sarah was partial to pastels.

The light breeze swayed the planter hanging by the corner of the garage, sending the sweet fragrance of petunias through the air.

Should he text her or just knock? He swiped his fingers over the nervous beaded moisture on his brow.

Mark wandered to the end of the driveway and looked up and down the street. Women liked to take their time getting ready, didn't they?

It was ridiculous for Mark to be so anxious. He didn't know what to expect since he hadn't seen Sarah since attempting to kiss her in the workroom. It had just felt so good, being with her, he'd gotten a little carried away by the moment.

The weather was perfect for their outing, seventy degrees with a light breeze. He leaned against the back rubber bumper. Sarah hadn't been back in the store since the night they'd almost shared a kiss. Each evening he'd waited for her to walk through the door. When she didn't, the night seemed endless even if he was busy. Although she did text him, saying she'd taken on a project at work and had been putting in long hours. He hoped it was true and she wasn't uncomfortable and avoiding him.

"Mark?" Sarah stood beside the pickup. "What are you doing?"

Lost in his thoughts, he hadn't even heard Sarah approach the vehicle. He straightened and felt beads of moisture dot his forehead and upper lip. "I was early." He knew his grin was sheepish.

Sarah laughed. "I've been ready for an hour." She picked at a white thread on her lime-green-and-white-striped T-shirt that matched the cuffs on her green shorts. "So to pass time, I worked on my quilt blocks." She stuck the errant thread in an outside pocket of her purse.

"Guess that means we're both ready to get this date started, then." Mark took her hand, guided her to the passenger side of the pickup, and opened the door.

After sliding into the driver's seat, Mark eased the pickup from the driveway.

"We match today." Sarah waved her finger back and forth between them.

Her pleased expression made Mark glad that he'd chosen the lime-green-and-white-plaid shirt.

"I got the dress code memo." Mark winked at Sarah before he pulled away from the stop sign, glad that Sarah lived on the same side of town as Falls Park. If he calculated correctly, they'd be there in fifteen minutes.

Sarah squealed when the opening bars of a pop song drifted through the pickup cab. "I haven't heard that song since high school."

"Me, too." Mark increased the volume a bit. "I pay for multiple stations on my XM radio but seldom change it from the eighties music."

Sarah joined in on the chorus of the song and tapped her hand on her knee. "That takes me back to my high school days."

Mark adjusted the volume to allow for easier conversation. "You do feel up to a stroll through the park today?" If Sarah's MS symptoms were bothering her, she might prefer to catch a movie instead.

"Oh, yes, I need some fresh air."

"Me, too. I've been cooped up in the store too much this week. The long hours coupled with the perfect weather, I've been anxious to be outside, connecting to nature."

Once they were parked, Mark quickly exited the vehicle and rounded the back to help Sarah out of the high four-wheel drive, glad he'd purchased the model with built-in running boards since Sarah was so petite. Although it might be nice to hold her waist and lift her out to the ground, Mark held his hand out for Sarah to grasp for balance as she eased from the seat.

"This was my very first indulgence after my mom passed away." The horn on the pickup honked as he hit the Lock button on the key fob. "I'd always driven a van with handicap capabilities to make it easy for Mom." Why had he shared that? It was Sunday afternoon all over again, when his first thought was to call Sarah after his employee quit.

"It sounds like you were a good and dependable son." Sarah laced her fingers in his and gave his hand a squeeze.

I had to be—she didn't have a good and dependable

husband. Mark sighed. He was losing sight of his dating strategy with Sarah. Something he couldn't afford to do because he'd never want to hurt her. Yet he was a Sanders man. He'd seen firsthand how reliable they were. He didn't quite understand some of his feeling regarding Sarah, but he had to get back to his original plan. That included getting her to talk about her breakup so she could let go of the hurt.

"Tell me, Sarah, how a beautiful woman like you has managed to be unattached?" Mark steered them toward the roar of water on the falls.

Sarah's shrug pulled their joined hands up. "Never met the right guy, I guess. The older I got, the less I dated."

Sarah's wistful expression of love gone wrong twisted Mark's heart.

"As a matter of fact…" Sarah took a deep breath before finishing.

Here it comes, her first step in letting go of the old boyfriend.

"This is hard to admit, but this is the first date that I've had in three years."

"What?" That blew his dating theory out of the water.

When Sarah stopped walking and stared at him, he realized he'd verbalized part of his thought.

Mark stopped short. "I'm sorry, Sarah, but you're gorgeous. I guess I figured you'd have your choice of suitors."

Sarah lifted her right hand to her chest. Her eyes sparkled like the sunshine-kissed water going over the falls. Her features softened with her gentle smile. "Thank you."

Her ragged whisper of gratitude tugged at Mark's heart. It took all of his willpower not to pull her into his arms and kiss her.

Mark followed when Sarah began walking again. "I wasn't dating anyone when I was diagnosed with MS, and at the time, I thought not being in a relationship was for the best. I knew I had to come to terms with the disease before I could commit to anything else."

"When did you find out you had MS?" Mark swung their joined hands.

"About eighteen months ago. It bothered me quite a bit at first because of some of the changes the doctor told me to make, but I have a handle on it now." Sarah sighed. "I just wish my mom and longtime friend thought I did."

It clicked. Mark stopped walking, halting Sarah with a slight tug on her hand. He gazed out at the falls. The rushing waters roared over the rocks then dropped into a foaming pool before continuing on their journey. The breeze lifted the spray, misting the air and dampening their faces. Sarah was upset about a relationship breakup, just not the kind Mark thought.

"Mom's supportive to an extent. My friend Karla isn't at all. She wouldn't even pledge me for the MS walk." Sarah voice didn't hide her disgust with her friend. "They both think I do too much. When I had to change occupations, they thought I rushed into the first job that hired me. They think I should work part-time, not have any hobbies, not be involved in any organizations."

Anger burned inside of Mark. He'd witnessed that so many times with his mother. He'd like to meet those women and tell them a thing or two. Having multiple sclerosis didn't mean you had to quit living. The person fighting the lack of muscle control needed to be supported, not discouraged. Mark checked his anger. "Don't let them get to you." He slipped his arm around Sarah and hugged her close.

Sarah leaned into him. "Sometimes it's hard not to, but I refuse to be defined by my disease."

Mark released the hug and cupped her face in his palms. He tilted her head up and drank in the determination that flashed from her eyes. The breeze ruffled her fringe of bangs as he traced his spread fingers up the soft curve of her cheeks, grazing the silky hair cut just above her ears.

The thunder of his heart drowned out the crash of the water on the rocks of the falls. Sarah shouldn't be fighting this battle alone.

Sarah rested her hands on his forearms. The slight squeeze of her velvet touch signaled her consent to the kiss. Her eyes fluttered shut as he closed the small gap between them and captured her lips.

He'd intended to kiss Sarah today. He'd intended it to be a good-night kiss. He'd intended it to be short but sweet.

However, Sarah needed to know that someone supported her and wanted to protect her from the cynics in the world. An intense emotion welled inside him and, when their lips touched, spilled over into the kiss, surpassing the innocent I-had-a-good-time-today message he'd intended to convey at the end of the date.

Instinct took over as Mark deepened the pressure and dropped his hands from her face and wrapped them around her shoulders. He needed to tell her that he'd be her shelter, the one who'd help handle her problems. *Yeah, right*.

The subconscious thought triggered the realization of what he was thinking. Mark ended the kiss and drew a ragged breath.

Raw feelings showed in Sarah's dark eyes as she searched his face.

That was not a part of his dating plan. What had he done?

The brooding began the minute Mark told Sarah good night on Saturday night. It was the only way he could control his giddy feelings caused by one fantastic kiss.

Mark stopped shelving fabric bolts and pursed his lips to remove the smile brought to his face by the previous thought. A repeat of the afternoon kiss couldn't happen again and it hadn't.

When they'd reached Sarah's door, she turned in an expectant manner. "Mark, this was a wonderful day." The light from the full moon couldn't compare to the radiant happiness shining from Sarah.

He'd known he couldn't repeat the same mistake as earlier in the day. Maybe if he didn't touch her soft ivory skin. It took all his willpower, but he stuffed his hands in the front pockets of his shorts.

As he leaned in, Sarah rested her hands in the exact spot they'd been earlier in the afternoon. The same quaking from her touch vibrated through him. It took all of his willpower, but he managed a chaste good-night kiss, which lasted about two seconds. Who knew love's electrical current didn't need much time to shock happiness into a heart?

The full moon magnified Sarah's beauty as her trust-filled eyes searched his face. She didn't seem to mind the quick peck, judging by the breathless sound of her voice as she said good night.

Mark sighed. It tore him in half trying to ward off the happiness with the brooding. Yet sooner or later he'd let Sarah down. He knew that. It was in his genetics.

On Sunday, Sarah called to thank him again for the nice afternoon and evening. He'd hoped she was stopping by the store to practice sewing, but she had a church committee meeting later in the day. Then yesterday, she ended up having to work late, so she couldn't spend the evening sewing in the workroom.

Here it was Tuesday evening, and no matter how hard he tried, the anticipation of seeing Sarah was bringing out the joy of that kiss.

Mark noticed a bolt with under a yard of cloth wrapped around it. He pulled it from the shelves to cut it into fat quarters.

"I'm back from dinner, so go anytime." Terri walked to the cash register area.

"In a minute." Mark put the fabric bolt under the cutting counter as he glanced at the clock. Sarah should have been here by now. He pulled his cell phone from his pocket. Had he missed a text? They'd planned to share dinner before the class.

Mark walked to the front plate-glass windows and scanned the parking lot for Sarah's compact.

"A watched pot never boils."

What was Terri talking about? Surely she didn't know he was worried about Sarah. He turned. "Pardon me?"

Terri laughed. "That's what my grandma would say if

we watched out the window for our dad to arrive home. I thought it was appropriate. The customers won't come in any faster for the Tuesday night sale with you watching out the window."

Mark grinned. "I guess not." He'd forgotten about his Tuesday night promotion.

When he turned back to the window, he noticed that Sarah had parked in front of the door and was walking around the front of her car. Really, she was limping while holding on to the hood of the car.

At the jangle of the quilt shop door, she turned before stepping from the curb. The soft light of dusk didn't mask the dark circles under Sarah's eyes. That, coupled with the limping, told Mark that her MS was acting up.

"Hi." Her voice sounded brighter than he thought it might as she continued to steady herself with one hand on the car. She held her free hand out to him.

Mark ignored her hand and pulled her into a side hug. "Hi." She leaned into him, and the warmth of her body comforted his longing to see her. "Let me get whatever you're after."

"It's my tote bag, purse, and our dinner."

Mark gathered the bags as quickly as he could. He could tell that she needed to sit down. He manually locked the car door before joining her on the curb.

He held his hand out to her, but she waved him off. "Just get the door, okay?" Sarah smiled, but Mark could tell that it took concentrated effort for each small step she made toward the door.

Mark opened the door, and Sarah made it through. She was still dressed in her office attire—a blue ruffled blouse under a short-sleeved white linen pantsuit—and the blue-and-white strappy slip-on sandals weren't helping with her footing.

Once inside the door, he offered his arm, and this time Sarah accepted. "I hope you like chicken. I bought grilled and extra crispy."

Even tired and bothered with MS, Sarah worried about others.

"I like both and it smells really good."

Sarah flicked on the workroom light. She let go of Mark's arm when they were close to the table. "Do you mind taking my stuff to the machine I use?"

"Not at all." Mark set the bag of food on the table and watched Sarah drop onto a chair.

"It feels so good to sit down. I've been running all day." Sarah lifted her right leg with both hands and rested it on the metal support bar underneath the table.

"I hate to tell you this, but it shows." Mark unpacked the food. "Sarah, with MS you need to rest. Mom took a nap almost every afternoon."

Sarah frowned. "I don't have that luxury. Your mom ran her own business." Her answer was clipped.

"Don't you have a lunch hour? You could rest in the break room." Mark dished food onto two paper plates and slid one in front of Sarah.

Sarah dropped her gaze. "I've been too busy to take a lunch the last two days."

"Sarah—" Mark stopped when she held up her hand.

"It's only because it's the start of this construction project. You know with contractors you are at their mercy for time schedules. It's not like I'm not eating. I eat piecemeal in between crises."

"Still, you should get away from your desk for a few minutes, especially since you've been putting in long hours." Mark removed another drumstick from the cardboard container and placed it on his plate before forking a bite of mashed potatoes.

"Can we talk about something else?" Sarah's eyes brimmed with tears. "I spend so much time dealing with renovations that I'm dreaming about them." Sarah tasted a tiny bite of potatoes before pushing them around on her plate.

"Okay, how did your church meeting go?" Mark took a bite of his drumstick.

"Great." Sarah's eyes lit up. "Not only am I leading the summer early bird Bible study group, but I'm also on a committee to review the curriculum for children's and adult Sunday school."

Mark grimaced before he could stop it. Her schedule was too demanding for a person with MS.

Sarah's sigh held a tone of disgust. She placed her fork, which was still holding a piece of chicken on which she'd been nibbling, atop her napkin and worried the hoop earring in her left ear. "What's wrong with that?" Defiance flashed through Sarah's dark eyes.

"Nothing, if you have the time, but do you?" Mark held her gaze. It was obvious she didn't like this conversation, but he knew firsthand the punishment MS could dish out.

"This remodel project won't last forever. Once I get the bids and know we're within budget and the client is getting what they want, then my work hours will go back to normal."

The corners of Sarah's mouth drooped as she narrowed her eyes at Mark. "Excuse me." The metal chair legs scraped across the tile floor as Sarah pushed away from the table.

Mark stood. "Sarah, I didn't mean to make you angry. I just want you to understand that leading an active life is not the same as leading a busy life."

"Active and busy are the same thing." Sarah rose from her chair.

Mark walked around the table. "Please sit down and enjoy your dinner."

"I'm behind on my quilt blocks, so I need to work on them *now*." Sarah started to turn away.

Mark saw the wobble. His stomach clenched. "Sarah, stop." He bumped his hip on the corner of the table, trying to get to her before she tried another step.

Sarah's eyes widened, her left arm reaching, missing the chair and knocking it off balance.

Mark seemed to be moving in slow motion while Sarah moved in real time. Her arms flailed in the air. He wasn't going to get to her in time.

The clang of the metal chair hitting on the tile floor muffled her cry as she started to fall.

Chapter 8

Two quick steps for momentum before Mark twisted his body sideways. He straightened his right leg as he dropped to the floor. His left hip and bent leg absorbed the shock as he thudded against the tile floor. Jarring waves of aftershock traveled up his spine, rattling his teeth.

His right shoulder smacked hard against the floor, and he strained to keep his head from the same fate. His vision blurred. He fought the urge to close his eyes and succumb to the pain.

Mark hadn't slid for home base in thirty years, but the maneuver worked. Seconds after he made contact with the floor, Sarah's head and torso bounced against his chest, knocking any remaining air from his lungs. He wrapped his arms around Sarah and held on tight. He'd done it. He'd cushioned Sarah's fall.

Laying his head against the cool tile, Mark sucked in

air that his lungs puffed out as rapidly as he breathed it in. In between breaths, he huffed, "Are you all right?"

"I think so."

The catch in Sarah's voice said differently.

He drew a steadying breath and pushed himself up with one arm. The other arm remained around Sarah, holding her close. When had that happened?

Sarah struggled but with his help managed to guide herself into a sitting position. "My leg must have fallen asleep."

"Sarah, I think it was more than that." Though it pained him to do it, Mark's tone turned stern.

Shrugging from his embrace, a slight pout marred Sarah's features as she turned away from him. The burning pain in his left hip was no match for the agony seizing his heart. He'd hurt Sarah. Yet he wouldn't pull the words back, even if he could. What if that had happened to Sarah and she'd been alone? She needed to heed the warning symptoms of her MS.

Mark grasped the end of the table and pulled himself upright. He bent to help Sarah up, but she flailed her left arm at him.

"Maybe it was my shoes. I've had trouble walking all day." Sarah struggled to lift herself from the floor.

Ignoring the pain in his right shoulder, Mark scooped Sarah from the floor, one arm around her waist, the other under her knees. He set her on the table.

"First things first—did you get hurt?" He patted the arm of her jacket with his fingers to remove some gray dust she collected on her way down. He lifted her chin and looked directly into her eyes. "Be truthful."

Sad resignation crossed her features. "I don't know for sure. All I feel is tingling in my right arm and leg."

"Well, I'm taking you home."

"I want to stay for class. I'm already behind."

"Sarah, you need to rest. You can't keep going on this way. Do you really think that you can sew in this condition?" He'd seen that the control in her right arm wasn't at full capacity when she fell.

She shrugged.

"I'm taking you home. End of discussion." Mark hated to see Sarah's deflated demeanor, but she needed to stop overdoing it. He started to gather up their dinner. Sarah'd barely touched hers, so he'd make sure she heated it up at home.

"You can't take me home. I need my car to get to work tomorrow. I'm feeling much better anyway. By the time I sit through class, I'll have rested and will be able to drive myself home." Sarah slid from the edge of the table.

Tentatively, she put her left foot on the floor and then tested her right foot as if she were dipping it into a swimming pool to check the water's temperature. Taking in her subtle movements, Mark could tell her right leg was leaden.

"I'll be right back." Mark moved a chair closer for Sarah. "I'm going to tell Terri that I'll be gone for about an hour. Is there anything in your car that you need?"

"No." Sarah didn't disguise her terseness. "Really, Mark, I want to stay."

"I know that you want to stay, but you're not going to. You need some rest. While I'm talking to Terri, why don't you call someone to meet us at your house to stay with you tonight?"

Sarah's eyes grew wide, and her mouth gaped open at Mark's commanding tone. He'd hurt her feelings. The thought caused his heart to twist. It took all of his resolve not to cave in with an apology allowing her to stay.

"This is in your best interest." Mark purposely softened his tone. "I'll be right back to help you gather your things and take you home." He kept his eye on Sarah until he passed through the workroom door.

It surprised Mark to find a half dozen customers milling around the quilt store. He waited until Terri finished ringing up a customer, explained the situation, and headed back to the workroom.

Sarah hobbled from table to table. Her eyes met his when he came into the workroom. Mark crossed his arms over his chest and rocked back on his heels.

"My leg feels better, but you're right. I need to go home." She looked down at her pants leg. "Must have happened when I fell."

Mark saw the long rip in the leg of her outfit. "Are you sure you're not hurt from the fall?"

Sarah shook her head. "Only my pride. Thanks for catching me. Did you get hurt?"

"Judging by the burning pain in my thigh, I'm pretty sure I'll have a whopper of a bruise." Mark smiled at Sarah. "But I'll live. My truck's parked in back."

Mark gathered the same load of bags that he'd carried in from Sarah's car. He crooked his elbow. Still unsteady on her feet, Sarah slipped her hand through the opening and gripped his bicep as they made a slow journey to Mark's pickup parked in the back lot.

Mark opened the passenger door.

"I've got it." Sarah stepped onto the wide running board with her left foot and grabbed the handle attached just above the side window.

When she wobbled, Mark gripped her waist and

steadied her; then she continued to maneuver her body into the seat.

Moments later, Mark had only driven a few blocks when he realized that Sarah was dozing, her head leaning against the window. What drove her to take on so much? Determination was an admirable quality but not to the extent Sarah was taking it.

At the stoplight, Mark turned to check on his passenger. Her soft, even exhales briefly fogged the passenger window. Her relaxed features showed no sign of stress. When the light turned green, the slight acceleration swirled the cool evening air through his open window. Was it too cold for Sarah?

He brushed her lower arms with his fingers, intending to check her skin temperature. Instead, it roused her from her slumber.

"Are we at my house already?" Sarah yawned and stretched then reclined her head against the headrest, facing Mark.

"Just about. Did you find someone to come and stay with you?"

After a few moments of silence, Mark glanced toward Sarah. Had she fallen back to sleep?

Sarah's eyes were wide open. "No, I didn't call anyone."

"Sarah, someone should be there with you."

"I know my parents or Karla would come, but—" her tired sigh showed her weariness "—I'm not up to the lecture that would accompany their help."

"Lecture?"

"They all think that I'm doing too much. Well, Karla doesn't think I understand the severity of my illness."

Anger flared in Mark, that Sarah's loved ones would

lecture her when she didn't feel well. Didn't they under-stand that someday she might need their help getting dressed or in and out of a car? Mark's knuckles whit-ened as he gripped the steering wheel.

Sarah sighed as he turned into her short driveway. "They don't understand that, like Job, I'm taking the bad with the good in my life."

That explained Sarah's interest in the Job's Tears quilt block and why she signed up for a quilting class when she didn't know how to sew. Mark's anger at Sarah's support system died down to a smolder of an-noyance. He wasn't quite sure that Sarah's interpreta-tion of her problems mirrored Job's struggles. Job did nothing to bring on his suffering, and although Sarah did nothing to bring on the MS, she wasn't being very smart about the management of her disease.

Sarah needed to relax more. He suspected she started the quilting class for that purpose only to find it more stressful because she lacked sewing abilities.

"I wish you'd have called someone, but since you didn't, I'll stay long enough for you to get settled in for the night." As Mark parked, slipped from the pickup, and rounded the front, he chided himself for not staying in the workroom to make sure Sarah made the phone call.

Sarah opened the truck door and, with the help of the dashboard and headrest, turned in the seat. "I will be fine—" Sarah enunciated each word "—tonight, to-morrow, the next day."

She tried to slide from the passenger seat, but Mark blocked the open space with his body. He cupped her face in his hands. "I know you will because I'm going to see to it."

* * *

Mark arose early the next morning so he could pick Sarah up for work since her car remained in the parking lot in front of his store where it'd stay today. He'd devised a plan after he left Sarah's house the night before.

Slipping the earpiece of his phone into place, he commanded, "Call Sarah."

"Good morning, Mark." Some of the weariness in Sarah's voice had disappeared, probably due to a good night's sleep.

"Good morning. I'm on my way to your house to pick you up for work but just realized that maybe you don't feel like going into work today and want to call in sick."

"Of course I'm going to work today. I'm in the middle of compiling and finalizing remodel bids." Sarah didn't disguise the "duh" factor in her voice.

Mark ignored it and continued with his plan. "Have you eaten breakfast yet? I haven't and thought maybe we could swing through a drive-through on the way to your office." At least he'd know that she ate something.

"Oh, an egg sandwich sounds good." Her voice brightened.

"I should be there in fifteen minutes. Will you be ready?"

"Yes. See you in a few." Sarah giggled before she ended the call.

Instead of lecturing Sarah, like her family, about her overdoing, he'd figured an alternative approach might be more beneficial. Today, by driving her to work, he'd make sure she didn't have to fight rush-hour traffic and ate a good breakfast. There'd be no working late tonight because without a car, she'd be dependent on him to get her back to the quilt store. Since Terri's shift ended at six, Sarah would be forced to leave at quitting time.

He couldn't control her lunchtime for relaxing, but he'd make sure she had a relaxing dinner even if it was eaten in the workroom of the store with her feet propped on a folding chair. He didn't have all the details worked out, but he knew that his work schedule allowed him two days to surprise her with a lunch date. Again, she might not be napping to ward off the fatigue that accompanied MS, but she would be resting.

Mark pulled into her driveway. Before he could exit his vehicle, Sarah came out of her front door. She sported the yellow crop pants outfit that she wore to the first quilting class. She balanced her tote bag on her left shoulder. Mark saw the subtle drag of her right foot as she walked toward the pickup. Her shoe choice, sturdy low-heeled sandals that buckled just under her ankle, suited her disease better.

Mark exited his pickup. "Let me get that for you." He took her bag. The pleasant flowery scent that he'd come to associate with Sarah tickled his nose. He inhaled deeply as he slipped his hand in hers. "Not only do you look terrific, you smell good, too."

"Thank you." When Sarah giggled, light danced in her eyes, even though dark smudges remained under them. Hopefully, his plan would work and fatigue's telltale signs would be gone by the end of the week.

On Saturday morning, Sarah waited for the barista to fill her order. She felt great. The problems with the construction blueprints started to diminish by Friday, which pleased her boss because of building costs and left Sarah's shoulders lighter without that burden of responsibility.

Mark surprised her for lunch two days in the past week and met her for dinner two nights. Sarah rolled her eyes. Being a typical man, he always brought or ordered too much food and insisted she take it home. Which was okay—less cooking and cleanup time involved in reheating leftovers, plus she enjoyed thinking about him while dining on his entrée.

A garden club event kept her mom in Brookings, so Sarah slept late then puttered around her apartment until after lunch. Now she intended to surprise Mark with a sweet treat then work on her quilt blocks.

Carrying a pressed-board tray—loaded with two coffees, a slice each of lemon poppy seed and banana bread—in one hand and her tote bag and purse in the other, Sarah walked to Granny Bea's. She stepped aside to allow a customer to exit and slipped in the open door.

Something was wrong. Mark's hair fell to the side, exposing some thinning on top. His light blue polo shirt was nearly untucked from his cargo pants on his right side, and his reddened face looked, well, harried.

Mark measured then cut fabric as he chatted with a customer. Several other people milled about the store.

Slipping the coffee tray and bag on a shelf under the cash register, Sarah wandered to the middle of the store. When she caught Mark's eye, he did a double take then sent her a weary smile. A disheveled stack of fabric bolts lay at the unused end of the cutting counter.

She turned a small circle on her heel, looking around the store. No sign of Terri or her daughter. Two carts full of patriotic material sat alongside empty shelving near the front of the store. Sarah walked over to it and found one cart actually held two neatly folded quilts.

Waiting until Mark finished ringing up his customer, she strolled toward the cash register with knitted brows. "What's going on here?"

"Illness struck at Terri's house. She and her daughter both have strep throat. Poor gals. Terri's voice is so raspy I could hardly understand her. But that leaves only me on a Saturday, of all days." Mark ran his fingers through his hair, the gesture explaining today's tousled hairstyle.

"Well, I put a treat under the counter for you, if you have time."

Mark lifted a cup of coffee and sipped it. "You might not believe this, but this is only my second cup of coffee today." He peeked into the bag and withdrew the banana bread. "I haven't eaten since breakfast."

Sarah watched as Mark inhaled the sweet treat. "What can I do to help?"

"Nothing. You came here to practice." Mark nodded toward the tote bag dangling from her arm as he handed her the second coffee and the bag.

Sarah pushed the bag back toward Mark. "I think you need that worse than me. Save me the calories."

"You don't have to worry about calories, Ms. Buckley." Mark winked. "But you also don't have to tell me twice that it's mine. I'm starving."

"Look." Sarah leaned on the counter. "I know I can't help on the register or the cutting area without training, but I can finish that display over there."

A hesitant look crossed Mark's features. He popped the rest of his lemon bread in his mouth and ran his fingers through his hair again. "I don't know. This is your day off."

"What does that have to do with anything?" Sarah wrinkled her brow.

Minutes passed before Mark audibly exhaled. "Okay, arrange it however you want."

Sarah celebrated with a victory fist, which brought a gleam to Mark's eyes.

"Hand me your tote, and I'll stow it under the register. But if you get tired, go back to the workroom and rest." Mark gave her a stern look and pointed his index finger at her. "I mean it."

"I will, don't worry." Sarah turned on her heel and headed toward the display area in the front of the quilt shop.

As she studied the Peg-board that hung above the three-by-three-foot shelf, she determined that the quilts should be hung on the Peg-board above the fabric. It would be easier to hang the quilts before she shelved the fabric bolts. Sarah moved the sturdy step stool to the shelf and began to hang the first quilt.

"Excuse me."

Sarah looked down at an elderly lady.

"Can you help me find this thread?" She held up the end sticker from a spool of thread.

After pushing another pin into the top of the quilt to hold it to the board, Sarah turned to find Mark. He was busy cutting fabric for a lady while another waited her turn. "Sure." Sarah climbed down from the step stool and took the offered spool information.

"Even with my glasses that print is pretty small. I don't want to get the wrong color."

Sarah led the way to the thread display, chitchatting

all the way about the lady's quilt project. Sarah located the brand and color family before perusing the spools for the numeric code. "Here you go."

"Thank you."

As the woman walked away, Sarah went back to the display. During the next two hours, Sarah either assisted customers with simple requests or listened to their suggestions about the display she'd assembled. All the conversations warmed her heart and reminded her of the reason she'd loved her UPS delivery job so much—the varied conversations.

Mark approached the seasonal display just as Sarah was putting on the finishing touches. With his hair neatly combed straight back and his polo shirt now tucked into his sand-colored cargo pants, he'd lost the frazzled look from earlier in the day. Sarah thought Mark's hair combed this way complemented his eyes, yet she found him very attractive when his hair feathered across his forehead, as it had earlier in the day. Her fingers itched to ruffle his hair back up so it fell across his forehead in a tangled mess.

"I think you missed your calling. That's a great display." Mark studied both sides of the shelving and Pegboard. He crossed his arms over his chest and rocked back on his heels. "This is an excellent idea." Mark waved a finger at all the red, white, and blue sewing accessories Sarah had arranged across the top of the flat framework of the shelf.

A thrill of pride bubbled through Sarah at hearing Mark's praise of her work. "I was going to ask your permission to add all the patriotic-colored thread, yarn, and quilt binding over here, but you were busy with a customer at the time. I figured if you didn't like it, I'd just put it back where I found it." Sarah shrugged.

"Whew, we've been busy today. Murphy's Law. I guess I should be shorthanded all the time. It's pretty quiet now, though, so you go practice your sewing and relax. Help yourself to a soda in the small fridge in my office."

Sarah glanced around the store. Two customers perused the fabric. She'd had so much fun helping out in the store that she hated for it to end, but she needed to get to work on her Job's Tears quilt blocks. "I probably should. I'm really behind on assembling my quilt blocks."

She followed Mark to the register area where he gathered her bag from under the counter. "Can you stick around until dinnertime? I'd like to buy you dinner, that is, if you don't mind eating in the workroom again."

"I can and I don't." Sarah flashed a broad smile over her shoulder as she walked back to the workroom. She grabbed a soda and Mark's office chair from the darkened room adjacent to the workroom.

She arranged a folding chair so she could put her right foot up while she sewed. She'd have to try running the foot feed with her left leg.

A slight tingle had started in her leg as she'd finished up the display. She'd visited her MS doctor during the week, and he confirmed her suspicion—her MS now affected her right leg, too, a fact she planned to keep secret. She'd accepted her fate and knew that God was sending all her extra activities as the good to counterbalance the bad. She wished her family members felt the same way. She hated keeping secrets from them, but in a way she was sparing them and herself from more disagreements. What others didn't know wouldn't hurt them.

Chapter 9

Late Tuesday afternoon, Mark balanced on his haunches, storing extra thread in a lower cupboard. The door buzzer signal sped Mark's heart. Could it be Sarah? He glanced at his watch. Five o'clock. His heart rate returned to normal.

"Be with you in a minute!" Mark called, intent on finishing the task at hand. When all the boxes were stacked away in neat rows, his knees groaned with midlife stiffness as he pushed himself up onto his feet. He scanned the store but couldn't see anyone.

Mark walked toward the front of the store and saw a stocky, white-haired gentleman beside the patriotic display, leaning on a cane. "Uncle Walter?"

Mark held out his hand as he approached his father's brother.

"Mark."

Walter's hand met Mark's, his uncle's handshake

firm, his uncle's eye contact deliberate, a holdover from his army days. Then Walter pulled Mark into a loose hug. Arm's length affection. It ran in the family.

"Nice setup you have here." Walter nodded toward Sarah's hard work. "Looks like something Gert would have put together. You must have inherited her artistic talents as well as her sewing skills."

Mark held his palms up. "I only sew enough to demonstrate the machines in the store. A friend of mine assembled the display, but I have to agree, it reminded me of Mom's work, too."

Walter met his eyes. "She was a good woman, your mom. Deserved better."

Mark's heart twisted, and instant moisture misted his eyes. He knew Walter wasn't referring to her MS. He swallowed hard but ended up answering his uncle with a nod. Walter patted Mark's shoulder then looked back at the display.

"I'm glad to see America being proud of her soldiers again. Greeting them at airports, holding celebrations."

Walter's wistful face held regret. Mark knew some of the returning Vietnam vets weren't showered with glory. He placed a hand on Walt's shoulder and squeezed.

"Well, I came here to ask you a favor. Is this a good time to talk?" Walter adjusted his glasses.

"Sure, if you don't mind talking on the sales floor. My sales help is at her dinner break." Mark crossed his arms and rocked back on his heels.

"Here's fine." Walter waved his hand in the air. "It's nothing that private." He lifted his quad cane. "Hip replacement surgery. I'm going to get rid of this."

"That's great. When?" Mark didn't remember his

uncle without a limp. During active duty, shrapnel had injured Walter's hip.

"I'm shooting for October, after the busy season at the hotel. I know it's early, but I wondered if you'd take me to the VA hospital and wait while I had surgery."

"You know I will." That was the downside of being a Sanders man—no woman to help them during the hard times. But then again, it was of their own doing. Probably in a few months, Sarah would just be a pleasant memory. The thought clenched Mark's insides. The truth hurt.

"Thank you. Now I'll get the date scheduled with a surgeon and let you know." Walter smiled.

"Excuse me a second." Mark saw Sarah through the plate- glass window and walked over to open the door.

"Thank you. I brought dinner." Sarah held up a bag from a grocery store deli.

"Smells great. Sarah, I'd like you to meet my uncle Walter." Mark guided Sarah by the elbow to where his uncle stood.

"Uncle Walter, I'd like you to meet Sarah Buckley." Mark relieved Sarah of her bags. "She's the one who arranged this display. Sarah, this is Walter Sanders."

Sarah met Walter's firm handshake and direct eye contact with a smile. "Do you like the patriotic arrangement?"

"Very much. You did a good job."

"Thank you. It was my first try. Would you like to stay and have dinner with us? There's plenty of food."

"Thank you for asking, but no. I want to get home before dark. You two go on and eat your dinner." Walter's cane rattled as he lifted it then thunked it against the tile floor as he took a step toward the door. "Good to know you." Walter nodded to Sarah.

Sarah reclaimed her bags. "It was nice to meet you, too." She wiggled her fingers at the men before turning and heading back to the workroom.

"Let me walk you out, Uncle Walter." Mark took short steps to keep the same stride as Walter. As they neared the front of the store, the door opened.

Mark and Walter paused as Caroline came into the quilt shop.

"Walter! How are you?" Caroline dropped the bags she carried and wrapped the man in a hug.

"Good." Walter patted her back. "How are you?"

"She's better than good—she's in love." Mark regretted the words as soon as he'd spoke them. Love and Sanders men just weren't a good mix.

Walter chuckled. "Congratulations, Caroline."

Caroline laughed.

"I can't believe you still hang around this guy after all the trouble he gave you growing up." Walter wagged his finger at Mark.

"The tables have turned. Now I give him trouble." Caroline continued to laugh as she picked her bags back up.

"It was nice to see you, Caroline. Mark, I'll be in touch."

Mark grabbed the door and held it open for his uncle. "Good-bye. Call me anytime."

"He looks good," Caroline said as she and Mark walked toward the back of the store.

"He's getting a hip replacement in October. He came to ask me if I'd sit at the hospital during his surgery." Mark sighed.

Caroline stopped walking. "Don't you want to?"

"Of course I do. It's just Uncle Walter's another reminder that Sanders men aren't good with relationships. They either leave or drive away women." Mark looked down at the toe of his scuffed loafers, not proud of the fact the same blood ran through his veins.

"Mark! You can't even compare Walter's situation with your father's desertion. Walter is a fine man."

What Caroline said was true, but what Caroline didn't say was true, too. His dad was a horrible example of a man, and that was whose blood coursed through Mark. His heart no longer pattered with happiness at seeing Sarah. This relationship was doomed to be short lived by genetics alone.

Until Caroline's soft fingers lifted his chin, he'd been so far into self-pity he didn't hear her bags rustle as she set them on the floor.

"Mark—" Caroline's tone now soft, soothing "—you and Walter are both Sanders men cut from the same cloth, fine cloth, good cloth, sturdy cloth. He is nothing like your father any more than you are. Don't ever forget that."

He searched her eyes and gave her a weak smile.

Caroline patted his cheek then picked up her bags and headed into the workroom.

Mark's gaze traveled to the plate-glass window, searching for another glimpse of Walter, who was probably long gone by now. Was Caroline right? Walter hadn't shirked his duty to his country, having intended to keep his promise of marriage to his fiancée. He'd stayed solid in times of trouble, unlike Mark's father. Walter's qualities reminded him of denim—tough, strong, enduring—whereas his dad's character was as thin as cheesecloth.

Caroline's words supplied the sunshine Mark's heart needed to let hope grow. He favored Walter's character. Why had he never seen that before? Mark had helped his mother through difficulties with her MS, he rode out tough business times, and, because he loved Sarah, for the past week he'd changed his plans to ensure that she took care of herself by getting plenty of rest.

It took Mark's mind a second to catch up with his heart. He smiled. He loved Sarah, and knowing that she had MS didn't change that fact one bit.

Sarah's stomach grumble insisted that it was past lunchtime. In fact, it was thirty minutes past her lunchtime. Interruptions drew Sarah away from compiling and printing out the rent bills, normally a two-hour job. She'd started that task first thing that morning and was now just finishing. As she folded the last rent billing and stuffed it into the envelope, the door to her office swooshed open. Her shoulders sagged—not another construction problem on the third floor. If so, it'd be three for three today. She tentatively raised her eyes.

"Hi, Sarah." Karla crossed the short space to the cherrywood desk.

Not a construction problem but an issue just the same. Sarah felt her shoulders sag further but forced lightness into her voice. "Hi, Karla, what brings you here?"

"Well, I was hoping that you had a minute to talk." Karla started to sit down in the reception chair.

"Wait." Sarah held up her hand to stop Karla. "Can we talk in the break room while I eat my lunch?" That way Sarah could confine the unpleasantness, which she was sure was coming, into a room where a client might not overhear.

"Sure." Karla smiled as she adjusted her purse strap on her shoulder.

Sarah slipped the phone earpiece from her ear and led the way to the adjacent room. "Have a seat." She pointed to the folding chairs beside the imitation-wood-grain table.

Once Sarah retrieved her sandwich, orange, and soda, she sat beside Karla. "How have you been?"

"Good." Karla smiled. "How about you? I haven't seen you in, well, forever."

More like three weeks, but who was counting? "I'm good but tired most days." Sarah saw Karla's instant frown. "I landed a big lease—the entire third floor. It requires a major renovation, so I've been putting in long hours here."

"So, you're finally around people more?" Karla searched her face. "Because you're such a people person, I don't understand why you'd want to work such a solitary job."

Karla's comment struck a chord inside of Sarah. Since she helped Mark that day in the fabric store, she'd really missed the variety of people she saw in her old job. Here, Ashley was the only person she really talked to. Other than saying good morning to other tenants, Sarah's encounters were brief and sporadic.

"Well, it's an adjustment, but then again, there's no heavy lifting and it's climate controlled, which helps my MS symptoms. I guess it's the bad that I have to take with the good." Hopefully, that should convince

Karla, although today Sarah had trouble swallowing Job's lesson.

Karla shrugged. "There are lots of jobs that are climate controlled where you'd interact with people all day. But if you like it, I guess..." Karla's voice trailed off as she looked around the bleak break room.

"I came here to give you this." Karla lifted her purse and unzipped the side pocket. She pulled out a check and handed it to Sarah. "My sponsorship for your MS walk."

"Thank you." The unexpected gesture cracked the wall Sarah had built around her heart where Karla was concerned. She gasped when she saw the amount. "This is very generous of you."

Karla shrugged. "It's the money I was saving for my trip to Europe. That isn't important anymore. I want them to find a cure for MS." Her gaze lowered, and her voice cracked. "I can't imagine life without you."

The defensive wall around Sarah's heart disintegrated. Had that been the real issue all along with Karla?

Sarah wiped the crumbs of lunch from her hands with her napkin then placed her hands over Karla's and squeezed. Karla finally lifted her gaze.

Sarah smiled. "Thank you very much. I'm sure it will help with research so all people who suffer with MS can lead fuller lives."

Karla nodded. "Now tell me what you've been up to besides working too much." Karla lifted her eyebrow to emphasize her last two words.

Today, the simple gesture warmed Sarah's heart instead of igniting her anger. "I volunteered to head the early bird Bible study through the summer, and in addition to my quilt class, I'm working on a committee to review church curriculum material."

Even as Karla's frown deepened the creases of her brow, Sarah defenses stayed in check.

"Sarah, you're doing more now than you did before your diagnosis. Are you sure that you aren't overdoing it?" Karla pursed her lips. "Do you allow yourself any time to rest?"

Sarah drew a deep breath. Mark worried about that, too. Couldn't any of them see how much happier she was now versus six weeks ago? When she had too much free time, it turned into a pity party about having MS and she'd have to push herself to leave her house to visit the quilt shop. Now, unless her symptoms flared up, she was so busy she seldom gave her MS a second thought.

"I'm fine, really," Sarah said, certain that reassurance was all Karla really needed.

The skeptical look Karla shot her made Sarah flinch, and defensiveness began to niggle her insides.

"At least the quilt class ends in a couple of more weeks. That should relieve some of your stress. How is it going, anyway?"

"Just a second and I'll show you." Sarah left the room to get her tote bag from her desk drawer. She pulled the completed blocks out as she returned to the room. "I planned to make a wall quilt, but I'm behind on sewing my blocks together." She placed six blocks in front of Karla. "I may be changing to the table runner."

Sarah sighed. When she did find the time to work on the Job's Tears blocks, she struggled with the lack of control from the MS in her arm, making the sewing even slower.

"I see improvement." Karla arranged the blocks side by side on the table.

"Thanks. I've found hand stitching the blocks works best for me." She paused, hoping Karla wouldn't say "I told you so" with her next admission. "And I'm also finding that I have to sew in spurts because of the MS in my arm, so it's taking longer than it should."

"Maybe I should have enrolled, and we could have made the quilt together since it seems so important to you." Karla started laughing. "Although my sewing wouldn't look any better than yours, and I don't have MS."

Sarah chuckled. "Remember those aprons we made in that home economics class we both hated?"

"Yes." Karla continued to giggle. "And they made us model those aprons in a fashion show. Embarrassing. That's why, for the life of me, I couldn't figure out why you enrolled in quilting class." Karla wiped at the corner of her eyes with the back of her hand.

"There was a reason." Finally, the conversation she'd been wanting to share with Karla for some time.

Karla sobered. "I know. You like the guy that runs the quilt shop. It's not like before, though, is it?"

"You mean one-sided interest?" Sarah searched her friend's face.

"No, I mean mixed signals. Sarah, I witnessed that married man talking to you, flirting with you, remember. I know your mom never thought so, but he led you on. You weren't wrapped up in some fantasy crush. He was a player. Please tell me that Mark isn't a player because—"

"I have the same look on my face when I talk about him?"

The astonishment on Karla's face pulled another laugh from Sarah. "Mom told me that."

Karla's features softened into a smile.

"One thing I know for sure is Mark isn't married. A family friend of his teaches the quilting class, and Mark introduced me to his uncle the other night."

"Okay, so he's not married, but that doesn't mean he's not a player and when your class is over you'll never see him again."

"Well…" Sarah wanted to jump to Mark's defense, but really, this was what she'd wanted Karla's reassurance on for a long time. "You tell me. He's always happy to see me. He's polite and treats me with respect. He compliments me, introduces me to people. We've only had one official date, but we spend a lot of time together. He drops by and brings me lunch and calls and text messages me throughout the day. He's always where he's supposed to be and, like you and Mom, he expresses his concern that I'm doing too much." Sarah stopped when she realized that she'd hardly taken a breath while she was ticking off Mark's attributes. Sheepishness stirred in her. "Sorry, I might have gotten a little carried away there. What do you think?"

"I think the only thing you left out is if he's a good kisser." Karla winked.

Sarah smiled broadly. "I don't kiss and tell."

Karla returned her smile. "He sounds like a great person. I hope to meet him soon, maybe at the MS walk?"

"You're coming to the walk?" Sarah clapped her hands together.

"Yes, to support you, encourage you, or just cheer

you as you finish." Karla stood. "I'd better let you get back to work."

Sarah walked her friend to the door. What an unexpected joy God sent her today.

Karla stopped in front of the door. She pulled Sarah into a tight hug. "I still think that you are overdoing things a bit, but Mark is good for you. Happiness surrounds you like a halo when you talk about him. I really hope he loves you as much as you love him."

There was no time to respond to Karla's statement before her friend disappeared out the door. Where did Karla get the idea that Sarah loved Mark? Sarah never mentioned it to anyone, even though it was true. She loved Mark.

"Am I glad to see you." Mark's expression showed his relief as he relocked the main door to the quilt shop. "I couldn't face another Saturday working alone."

"It's my pleasure, although I'm not sure how much help I'll be." Sarah stashed her purse and tote on the shelf under the cash register.

"Terri's family is sure having a run of bad luck. First strep, now food poisoning." Mark sighed and jerked his head toward the Help Wanted sign. "I guess it's just coming at a bad time for me."

"Well, I'm here now. Just show me what you need me to do." Happiness bounced through her since Mark phoned early this morning. As soon as he'd hung up with Terri, he'd called Sarah. His first choice. He needed her.

"I think you're here in plenty of time for some training. Measuring and cutting the fabric isn't that difficult, but there are some other things I'd like to run through."

"Okay." Sarah adjusted the ruffled collar of her light pink top. Glad she'd chosen it along with the white crop pants and flat tennis shoes. On the phone, Mark had said to dress casual, but she thought the tennies might be pushing it. To her relief, Mark also wore athletic shoes, jeans, and a white polo shirt with Granny Bea's stitched across the left side.

"I know it was hypocritical of me to ask you to come in and help me out in the store today when I'm telling you all the time that you overdo it. So, I'm insisting that if you get tired, you go rest in my office. I don't care how many customers are milling around the store."

Sarah's heart swelled with pride and love that she was the first person Mark turned to in his time of trouble. That seemed like a good sign. "I promise I will. But I feel great today. Obviously, you haven't had any luck hiring someone." Sarah pointed to the Help Wanted sign in the store window.

"I'm getting a lot of people who want to work certain part-time hours like afternoons or evenings. But the people who are flexible don't feel like a good fit for the store." Mark grimaced. "Sadly, I've been down that road, and it's easier to be under the stress of working alone."

Sarah closely watched as Mark demonstrated how to lay, smooth, and hold the fabric to cut it to ensure the accurate yardage. When it didn't take long for Sarah to catch on, Mark left her with instructions on cutting fat quarters while he ran down to the coffee shop for their breakfast.

After an hour of practicing cutting while Mark wrapped and marked the fat quarters, she felt confident she'd be an asset in the store. Time would tell, sooner rather than later. Mark flipped the door sign to Open and clicked the dead bolt.

Sarah continued to work on the fat-quarter task since Mark had fallen behind on that job in the last week. With each empty cardboard bolt she stacked in the cart beside the cutting table, a sense of accomplishment filled her. Similar to when she delivered parcels, and the piles became smaller and smaller.

Sarah's first customer test came about thirty minutes after the store opened. While Mark was busy showing a young woman the difference in the sewing machines, Sarah assisted a lady by cutting several yards of three different fabrics.

"What are you making?" Sarah wrote the number of yards on the preprinted form along with the price from the end of the bolt.

"This is backing for several quilt tops my church circle made. We're raffling one as a fund-raiser and giving the other two to the family that lost their home in a fire."

"What a wonderful idea. Will you get them quilted that fast?" Sarah measured a length of the fabric against the yardstick built into the counter. She repeated the process six times then smoothed the fabric and ran the scissors down the crevice in the countertop.

"We're tying the top to the back. That goes fast, and with many hands we'll get them finished in a couple of hours."

Sarah slid the folded cloth to the woman who then laid it in her cart.

"I'm not in a circle at my church, but I might steal your idea and see if the ladies in our circle will make a quilt and raffle it for a mission we sponsor in the fall." Sarah smiled. "We could choose a simple pattern."

"A nine patch sews fast."

"A nine patch." Sarah hadn't realized that she expressed out loud her mental note for the next committee meeting. Not knowing what that quilt design was, Sarah smiled at the lady. "I'll keep that in mind."

"Our circle made a pretty nine patch in red and green and backed it with poinsettia-printed fabric. We raised quite a bit of money with that quilt." The elderly lady's wide smile and twinkling eyes showed her love of quilting.

"Sounds lovely. Is there anything else?" Sarah smiled back at the lady.

"No thank you, dear."

"Good luck with your projects."

As the lady walked toward the cash register, Sarah rolled the bolts to tighten the remaining fabric. She heard Mark excuse himself from other customers so he could ring up the elderly lady's purchases.

Sarah looked up in time to see both Mark and the lady looking her way. The lady waved and headed for the door as Mark walked toward the cutting table. Sarah's stomach dropped. Had she done something wrong?

Mark shook his head as he crossed his arms over his chest; then he smiled. "That customer just told me that I should give you a raise." He gathered the bolts of material.

"What?" Sarah giggled. Then she knitted her brows. "You're teasing me. She didn't really say that."

"Yes, she did. She comes in here a lot and told me that even though you don't know what a nine-patch quilt pattern is, you're a very nice person and you'll learn." Mark chuckled.

Sarah laughed out loud. "Guess my expression showed my lack of knowledge."

Mark shrugged. "All that matters is she left happy. Keep up the good work."

Sarah watched Mark restock the fabric bolts before returning to the customer in the sewing machine area. She liked that Mark had shared his customer's compliment. She liked the cheery atmosphere of the store. She liked working with Mark.

After hanging up the phone with Mark this morning, she'd said a prayer for Terri and her family for better health. But Sarah almost hoped Terri needed another day of rest. It was fun working in the store. Sarah had forgotten how enjoyable work could be.

Chapter 10

Mark added more navy-blue thread to the accessories on Sarah's display. She'd done such a good job helping him out on Saturday and Sunday afternoon.

Unfortunately, he hadn't seen much of her since then. She texted him throughout the day, and they spoke briefly once each day over the phone. Her schedule this week was full. Too full for someone with MS, and he'd added to her burden, leaving her little time to rest.

He really hadn't expected her to come into the store to work last weekend. After he ended the call with Terri last Saturday, he'd dialed Sarah's number without thinking, because he had a problem and he wanted to talk to her. Actually, she was the one he wanted to share everything with these days.

That was selfish of him, because what free time Sarah had, she needed to use it resting, not helping him out.

The jangle of the door buzzer startled him, and he knocked over four spools of thread. He caught three before they hit the floor, but the fourth rolled away from him.

"Hi, Mark."

Mark looked up from his retrieval duties. "Hi, Diane. Did you come for my team information?"

"Yes, and I'll collect donations if you have any."

"I have a new team member for Gert's Gang this year—Sarah Buckley." Mark made a spool pyramid with the navy thread before he zigzagged around material displays to where Diane stood. "The information's in my office. I'll just be a minute."

Diane was leaning against the register counter when Mark returned with the MS walk packet.

She read the list of names on his envelope. "All the regular walkers plus one."

"That's right."

"Is Sarah Buckley a friend of yours?" Diane glanced up from the envelope.

Mark drew a deep breath. Although Diane had no problem telling him she was engaged, Mark found it hard to tell a former girlfriend that he was dating someone else. Generally, he never again saw the women he dated.

"By the twinkle in your eyes, I'd say more than a friend of yours. A girlfriend, perhaps." Diane's warm smile encouraged him.

"We've been dating. Nothing serious." The last two words rushed from Mark's mouth with practiced ease. Why did he say that? This time it wasn't true.

"Right, nothing serious." Diane lowered the envelope

then scanned the quilt store before looking directly into Mark's eyes. "Does she know that?"

"What do you mean?" He was always very forthcoming with his dating intentions. Had he been with Sarah?

"I mean, do your actions speak louder than your words? Are you saying you don't want a serious relationship—yet still doing all those little caring things you did while we dated, things that instill hope in a woman?"

Mark noted the slight edge in Diane's voice. Not quite sure what she alluded to, he crossed his arms over his chest and rocked back on his heels. With a grin, he kept his voice tone even and teasing. "Do I need to remind you that you broke our relationship off?"

Diane smiled sadly then shrugged. "No, you don't need to remind me. I thought if I broke it off, you'd have a change of heart—but you didn't." Sorrow infused her words.

She was serious. Is that what the other women had done, too? They hadn't gained self-confidence and planned to move on? Instead, they hoped by breaking it off, he'd come running back?

Diane laughed. "Your expression is priceless. You had no idea, did you? I wouldn't change one thing about my life right now, but Mark, you broke my heart. Just be mindful of this with—" Diane stopped and checked the envelope "—Sarah. Just be mindful of her feelings. They may be stronger than yours and, well…" Diane shrugged. "A broken heart's kind of hard on the self-confidence."

Mark felt like he'd walked behind a bowler who, just as the bowler swung the ball back for momentum on his roll, had clipped Mark in the stomach. Mark had broken Diane's heart, hurt her self-confidence. His body deflated. He was a Sanders man, through and through. "I'm s-s-sorry." Disbelief filled his words with the realization that his dating theory wasn't foolproof.

Diane adjusted her purse strap over her shoulder as she jutted out her chin.

The buzz of the air conditioner kicking on broke the thick silence in the store.

Diane fidgeted with the zipper tab on her purse. He'd broken her heart. What could he say to that?

"Well..." Diane sighed and turned to go.

Mark needed to say something. He caught her arm. "I am sorry, Diane. You're right. I had no idea that I hurt you like that. Please accept my apology." To how many other women did he owe this same courtesy?

Diane's lip curled into a sad smile. "I forgave you awhile ago, but I do accept your apology. Again, my life is better than I ever thought it'd be, but I've needed to hear that from you. I've needed that closure for a long time. So, thank you. And now maybe you could do me a favor."

"Anything."

"I know this is none of my business, but...don't hurt Sarah the way you hurt me." Moisture filled Diane's eyes, and she blinked rapidly before giving him a weak smile. "I guess I'll see you Saturday at the walk." She turned on her heel and headed for the door.

Mark watched Diane leave the store, then the parking lot. He stared blankly through the plate-glass store window. What had he done? Followed right in his dad's footsteps, that's what. He might not have been married to the women, but he deserted them in other ways. Was he giving Sarah false hope? When push came to shove would he back away from her?

Mark watched a cloud pass over the sun, blocking out its rays, just like Diane's admission covered his heart with sadness. How on earth did he think his dating plan was fair?

Lord, please forgive me for hurting all the ladies I dated in the past. I've been blind to the feelings of others, and I'm truly sorry.

He didn't deserve Sarah. Maybe he didn't deserve anyone. Sanders men just weren't dependable. Mark turned from the window. Yet he'd helped his mom run this store, and he didn't hesitate when Walt asked for his assistance earlier in the week.

He'd do right by Sarah even if it meant his heart got broken.

Would this light never change? Sarah rubbed her right arm, but it remained dead. Using her left hand, she moved her right arm to a comfortable position on the armrest. With difficulty she guided her car through the intersection, taking it slow for easier steering. Even though it was Saturday, she'd taken the long way to the park where the MS walk started, to avoid heavy traffic.

She yawned. What a busy week she'd had, but at least after this morning, she could cross one thing off her to-do list. By the afternoon, another item, the last curriculum meeting, would be marked off; then maybe she could get some quilt blocks sewn together. She flexed the fingers of her right hand as her arm rested. Hopefully, her medicine would kick in soon. She'd needed to refill her prescription but just couldn't work a stop at the pharmacy into her schedule this week. So she'd skipped her dosage a few days, to stretch her meds out until today when she could get to the drugstore.

Maybe she should have taken Mark up on his offer of a ride to the walk. The parking lot was packed. Awkwardly, Sarah turned her steering wheel with her left hand. Pulling her compact into one of the few remaining spots was tricky one-handed.

Sarah slipped from her car then zipped her car keys in the front pocket of her backpack. After several attempts to get her backpack in position with a numb right arm, she finally just inserted her left arm in the arm strap and let the backpack dangle at her side.

With each step toward the Gert's Gang gathering spot, Sarah's right leg tingled. She took deliberate and slow steps. Why of all days were these MS symptoms so intense? Mark waved as soon as he saw her. Caroline and Rodney turned and waved, too. Sarah straightened and tried to walk her normal stride but felt like her right foot was sliding into each step.

"Sarah, we were getting worried that you stood us up." Caroline patted Sarah's back as Sarah stopped by the group of people gathered around Mark.

"Here is a shirt for you." Mark held out a red MS walk T-shirt with the corporate sponsors listed on the back.

"I'm glad I wore navy yoga pants." Without thinking, Sarah tried to pull on the T-shirt. Her right arm failed to move in the direction it needed to.

Mark stared at Sarah. "Are you okay?"

"Just a little MS problem." Sarah forced a smile and wrestled with the T-shirt sleeve. "I think it's due to the unseasonable heat and humidity that blew in this week."

"Let me help." Mark took her backpack and guided her arm through the sleeve. He pulled the back of the T-shirt down while Sarah pulled the front. "Should you be walking today?"

Already annoyed with the flare in her MS symptoms, anger surged through Sarah. "I'm fine." She snapped the words as she fought back a yawn.

"Okay." Mark held up his hands in defeat then grinned. "I missed you this week."

His smile and words warmed her heart. "I missed you, too. I'm so behind on sewing my quilt blocks, but I've been working late and had two church meetings." Sarah tried to suppress another yawn but failed.

"Have you been getting enough rest?" Mark's beautiful hazel eyes were hidden as he narrowed his gaze on her.

"I went to bed late last night, that's all." She wasn't about to tell Mark that she'd been up past midnight every night this week. He was beginning to sound like Karla and her mother. She didn't need that today. It was taking every ounce of her strength to stand. She looked around for a bench. "I'd like to sit down."

"There's a chair over there." Mark crooked his elbow.

Praise God that Mark was a gentleman. Having him to lean on made her walking easier. She eased into the chair.

"Would you like some coffee? They have a stand over there." Mark pointed.

"I'd love some."

Sarah listened to the anxious chatter of the other walkers. She'd looked forward to this day, but now she felt too tired to enjoy it.

Mark handed her a cup of coffee then sat on the

ground next to her. "They have doughnuts, too. Would you like one?"

"No thanks." Sarah sipped the bitter beverage brewed stronger than she really liked.

"Is any of your family coming?"

Sarah rolled her eyes. "I doubt it. They aren't too supportive of my activities."

"I don't know two of the people who gave you very generous donations. I assumed the couple with your last name was your parents." Mark winked.

"Yes, the other one was my friend, Karla."

"Isn't she the one—"

"That thinks I'm doing too much? Yes, but then that seems to be the general consensus of everyone I know." Sarah looked pointedly at Mark.

His Adam's apple bobbed as he set his jaw. "Sarah, I think their concerns are valid. You don't rest enough. Fatigue is a huge issue for MS patients. You are overdoing it."

Sarah rolled her eyes. "I'm just proving that a person with MS can lead an active life." She let the terseness she felt flow into her words.

"The key word there is *active*. You are leading an *over*active life. I don't think I could keep the schedule that you do, and I don't have MS."

Sarah blinked. She'd never really considered that before. Had she been this involved in activities before her diagnosis? She'd worked overtime on her old job during the holiday season. She'd always been involved in at least one church committee. Really the only thing new was Mark, the quilting class, and the MS walk.

"Discouragement is not what I need today." Her own body's rebellion was enough to handle without everyone else thinking she should give up. But she'd learned from Job's story that if she trusted God, He'd help her to understand this affliction. See her through. After all, He'd already provided so many good opportunities for her that she shouldn't even be grumbling about her MS symptoms today. "I'm finishing this walk."

Mark pursed his lips. "Well, I'm staying right beside you. You do realize that I recognize the subtle MS signals that maybe your mom and Karla miss."

"Like?"

"The shuffle of your feet to hide the slight limp or sliding your feet along versus taking a step." Mark touched her forearm.

She pulled it away. "You are the one person I felt was on my side. Because of your mom I thought you understood how important it is for me to continue on with life as normal as possible." She tried to push off the chair, but her right arm slid off the canvas arm. Mark's strong arms stopped the chair's wobble.

"Sarah, let me help you." He stood to the side of the chair and wrapped his arm around her. She leaned into his warmth, and as he lifted, she stood.

"Thank you." Her appreciation came out more clipped than she'd intended, but she was tired. She was in pain. She was fed up with all the people wanting her to give up.

"I am on your side, Sarah."

Someone called Mark's name before she could respond. She pulled free of his embrace. "Go, where *you're* needed."

The immediate hurt that registered on Mark's face twisted her heart with regret. Yet the disappointment she felt in the knowledge that he agreed with her mom and Karla justified her remark. Maybe she was wrong that Mark cared for her.

"I'll be right back." Mark let go of her but kept his eyes on her as he walked away, no doubt looking for those telltale MS signs.

"A few of us are going to get started." Caroline stopped beside Sarah. "I'd ask you to join us, but I'm sure you're waiting for Mark." Caroline's blue eyes twinkled as she teased Sarah.

Sarah glanced to where Mark stood, his back facing her. "Actually, I'd like to get started. I'll join your group, and Mark can catch up."

With concentrated effort, Sarah bent down and picked up her backpack. Straightening, she brought up the rear of the small group of people. The short rest in the chair eased some of her symptoms. Although her arm ached, she felt she'd regained some of the control in her right leg. Not quite her normal gait, but she was keeping up with the group.

The sun blazed in the morning sky. She prayed that the front that moved into the area, bringing unseasonable mid-May warmth and humidity to South Dakota, would pass by this day. Her prayer went unanswered.

Although the temperature was actually a comfortable seventy-five degrees, the dew point made it feel more like eighty-five. Her sweat-dampened hair stuck to the nape of her neck. She raised her left arm and swiped the side of her face with her T-shirt sleeve. The weather fought against any good her MS meds were doing for her today.

Pain shot up Sarah's right leg with the next step she took. She grimaced but managed to stifle a groan.

"Sarah!" Mark's voice rose above the noisy laughter and chatter of the walkers.

She didn't want Mark to see her difficulty in walking. It took all her resolve to try to take a normal step. Whether anyone liked it or not, Sarah was like Job. She wanted to accept the bad with the good that God sent her way. Why couldn't others see their negative attitudes weren't conducive to her well-being?

"Sarah, wait."

Glancing over her shoulder, Sarah saw Mark jogging toward her. Once again, with concentration, she moved to take a normal step.

Her leg didn't cooperate. She started to wobble. The loaded backpack threw her balance off. She let it fall to the ground and tried to overcompensate, but with the lack of feeling in her leg she had no idea where to find her footing. She tried to throw her weight to the left, but the movement increased the speed of the fall. Her body pulled her backward. She closed her eyes and braced for the impact with the sidewalk.

"Oh." Mark's breath added additional heat to the back of her neck as her body knocked into his sturdy chest. He gently set her down on the sidewalk. "Are you all right?" He panted the words.

"Yes." Sarah's left leg was bent, and her right leg stuck straight out.

Members of the group she'd been walking with turned around when they heard the commotion. As a small crowd began to gather around her, humiliation stirred the embers of her anger into full-fledged flames. "Just help me up," she snapped.

"Not until I make sure you are okay."

Mark's terse tone turned her anger into rage. She struggled to get up, but her body wouldn't cooperate.

"You aren't going anywhere until the on-site paramedics check you out." Mark's firm grip held her in place.

She turned her head and glared at him. "Help me up."

His hazel eyes glared back at her. He clenched his teeth. "It's the walk's rules. I'll help you up after they check to make sure you aren't hurt." He tightened his hold on her arms. "If you're hurt, they'll take you the hospital. If you're not, I'm taking you home."

Sarah started to retort when two paramedics broke through the small crowd of people. After they shooed the people on, they went through a series of limb-movement checks. All they found was a cement burn on her left leg from her having grazed the cement on her way down.

After the paramedics cleaned then applied antiseptic to the abrasion, they set her in a wheelchair and suggested she let Mark push her for the rest of the walk. Sarah's humiliation deepened.

What a nightmare! She wanted out of this horrible chair. Why of all times had the weather heated up so early in the season and brought her such misery?

Mark sat in the grass beside the wheelchair and allowed the paramedics to clean the scrape that ran the length of his calf. Since the paramedics had first arrived, she'd avoided his gaze, but now she stole a glance his way. His face showed no emotion, and he laughed when the paramedic made a joke about the rescuer's injuries being worse than the rescuee's.

She should reach out, squeeze Mark's hand, and thank him for his help. After all, it was the second time he'd saved her from severe injury. But if she did it would seem like she'd be admitting defeat, especially after his change of attitude toward her active lifestyle. Mark stood and shook hands with the paramedics then turned to Sarah. "Where's your cell phone?"

His question confused her. Had he lost or broken his in the fall? "My backpack. Why?" She dug through the small area where she stowed her keys then held out her cell.

He shook his head. "Call someone—your mom, your friend, anyone, and tell them to meet us at your house."

"What?" Sarah's voice showed her surprise.

"We're not having a repeat of last time. You need someone at your house until you can get your MS under control. They need to make sure that you rest."

"I'm fine. It's just the heat." Sarah started to put the cell phone away.

Mark snatched it from her. "I'll do it, then. Who do you want me to call—your mom or Karla? It's not just the heat, Sarah. You have to scale back your activities. The long days at the office, followed by church committee meetings—they're adding to your misery."

"Give me my phone." Sarah reached in Mark's direction. He handed her the phone.

"And unfortunately, I've added to your stress, too, letting you help me in the store. I'm sorry for that. I knew better, and it won't happen again."

Bitter tears burned in Sarah's eyes. How could he take away the one thing she really liked, helping at the fabric store? "But I was just rescuing you those days, like you just did me."

Mark pursed his lips and shook his head. "Not the

same, Sarah. Please make the call so I can get you home."

"What if I don't want to go home? What if I want to stay for the entire walk?" She jutted her chin out in defiance.

"Fine, but you're spending it in the wheelchair." Mark positioned his stocky frame in front of her as if to block her escape. Right now, making a break for it seemed like a great idea.

Her gasp sounded far away and faint, like the last echo bouncing back to its caller. The sad reality snuck in. It didn't matter what her mind or spirit wanted—her body bound her to the wheelchair, holding her captive.

Her anger, instant and intense, caused her hands to tremble. She had no choice. Today she was dependent on Mark and whomever she decided to call. Why had this happened to her?

The urgent slap of sneakers on the cement drew Mark's attention from Sarah and gave him a second to compose himself. Her wounded expression twisted his heart in pain. He hated being stern with Sarah, but she obviously didn't comprehend the effects of MS on her body.

"Sarah, are you all right?" As she ran, the woman's purse swayed from her elbow then slapped into Mark's chest as she bumped into him when she squatted down in front of the wheelchair.

Sarah's lip quivered, but she squared her chin again.

"Did someone knock you down?" The woman grasped Sarah's hand.

Sarah's slight head shake removed the panicked concern from the woman's face. The woman's eyes narrowed, and Sarah took a sudden interest in her backpack.

Mark cleared his throat. "She fell."

The woman stood and raked her eyes over Mark. "Are you Mark?"

"Yes." Mark stuck his hand out.

"Karla." She clasped the hand he offered.

"I think Sarah was just about to call you."

They both turned to Sarah. She sighed and looked from Mark to Karla.

"My MS is really bothering me *today*." Her annoyance showed on the last word. "Mark feels that someone should stay with me for a while. Would you be able to spend a couple of hours at my house?"

"So you don't want to stay for the walk?" Mark wanted to verify her intention, since a few minutes ago she wanted to finish the walk.

Sarah yawned. "No. I want Karla to take me home." She flashed an indignant look at Mark.

"Um…" Karla looked at Mark and then Sarah. "I have to pick up my dog from the groomer in twenty minutes, but after that I'd be happy to take you home and stay with you."

Like a half-burned candle melting in a votive cup, Sarah dissolved in the depth of the wheelchair. She needed to get out of the hot, humid weather.

Mark frowned. "I'll take you home and wait until Karla can get there."

"Okay." Her meek voice revealed her reluctance to be dependent on others.

Mark hated seeing Sarah like this, probably just as much as she hated being in this situation. How could he make her see that some of her misery was self-inflicted?

Karla again kneeled in front of Sarah. "I'll stop at my house and pack a bag. We'll have a sleepover, just like old times. I'll pick up some lunch and treats. Is there anything special you'd like?"

Sarah dug through her backpack. She pulled out a pill bottle. "Can you stop and pick up my refill?"

"Sure." Karla took the bottle and put it in her own purse as she stood. "I'm leaving now. I'll see you at your house."

Mark watched Sarah pull a bottle of water from her backpack and struggle to remove the cap.

"I can do that for you." Mark reached for the bottle but backed off at the look Sarah shot him. "Let's get you home, then."

For once it paid for Mark to get to the walk site early. His pickup wasn't parked far from the starting point. He pushed the chair to the truck and angled it so he could open the passenger door.

In the second it took Mark to swing the door wide, Sarah had stood. "I don't think so." Mark admired Sarah's independent spirit, but ever since she'd fallen down, he'd wanted to scoop her into a tight embrace. The two quick steps it took Mark to get to Sarah seemed endless. He lifted her as if he would carry her across a threshold.

To his surprise she wrapped her arms around his neck, buried her face in his shoulder, and began to cry. Mark instinctively tightened his hold around her waist.

"Oh, Sarah." He managed to choke out the words around the lump in his throat before kissing the top of her head.

Sarah stiffened. Her hands pushed against his chest as she tried to sit erect in his arms. "Don't. Pity. Me."

Each word held a drip of venom like the fangs of a coiled rattlesnake.

What just happened? Mark searched Sarah's face. Though her eyes were red rimmed there was no mistaking the lick of anger flames flashing in her coal-colored eyes. "Sarah, I—"

"Put me in the truck." Even through clenched teeth, Sarah's words were loud and clear. She'd set her features as if she'd been etched in stone.

Mark obliged by lifting her onto the truck seat. He moved forward to assist in adjusting her to a more comfortable position.

"I've got it."

Mark wanted to help her. To defend himself. To protect her.

Instead, he backed away and closed the pickup door. He pulled the wheelchair back to the sidewalk, stopping by the driver's side. The weather was too hot for Sarah to wait in the vehicle while he returned the wheelchair to the paramedics.

He flicked the door handle and inserted his key in the ignition. A quick turn and the truck engine roared its start. He pressed the air-conditioning button and turned the fan to high. Sarah might not take care of herself to reduce her MS symptoms, but he could. He sneaked a glance Sarah's way. She wiggled herself back into the seat and snapped the safety belt.

"I'll be right back."

A snort of air was Sarah's indignant reply.

Mark shut the truck door, grabbed the wheelchair handles, and then hurried along the sidewalk, dodging other walkers, reporters, and onlookers. He'd envisioned this day much differently. A hand-holding, romantic stroll from start to finish, ending with a heart-to-heart talk over dinner, hoping he read her signals correctly and that she, too, wanted to take their relationship to a more serious level.

Obviously, he'd misread those signals. Why was he surprised? Didn't he recently find out that he'd broken many hearts along the dating path? Was the pain ripping into his heart right now payback for all the suffering he'd caused other women?

Mark handed off the wheelchair and thanked the paramedics for their help before turning back toward the parking lot.

Caroline's opinion about him being more like Walter than his father had hushed the warning voices inside Mark, causing him to let his guard down. Sarah's immediate rejection to his words of comfort separated the false happiness he held in his heart from the stark reality. He was a Sanders man. They didn't win in love.

The click of the pickup door roused Sarah from her quick nap. She lifted her sleep-laden lids, saw it was Mark, and then turned her head toward the side window and closed her eyes.

The low volume of the radio and Sarah's even breathing supplied white noise for Mark's thoughts as he drove across town to Sarah's house.

Her self-inflicted exhaustion and misdirected use of her meds had obviously caught up to her. Perhaps that drove her attitude today, mistaking his comfort for pity. His mom's MS fatigue made her cranky but not vehement. Something drove Sarah to overdo. But what? And more importantly, why?

Mark pulled into Sarah's driveway. They'd beaten

Karla. He pushed the gearshift into Park, killed the engine, and still Sarah didn't stir.

He knew she'd deprived herself of rest, so he wanted her to sleep as long as she could. Carefully he slid the backpack from her lap. Quietly he exited his vehicle, searched for her house keys, and unlocked the door.

Sarah's head still tilted sideways, her forehead resting against the side-window glass. He lifted the door latch and cracked the opening. He stuck his arm through the small space, held Sarah's shoulder, and then opened the door wide.

His touch startled her awake.

"You're home," Mark whispered. The softness of Sarah's skin invited his hand to stay put on her shoulder even as she straightened her head.

Sarah blinked several times like a sleepy child. The last blink uncovered the deepened anger that shone from her eyes. She'd gotten her bearings.

Her left hand swatted Mark's hand from her shoulder. "I think I can do this on my own." Sarah turned her frame until her legs dangled in the open doorway.

"Let me help you." Mark hovered at the edge of the pickup door, on alert for the first sign that a limb might inhibit her movement and knock her off balance.

"I don't need help." Sarah's voice shook as she spit out the words. She eased herself to the sidewalk and, holding on to the edge of the pickup bed, stood clear of the door.

Mark gave it a push, and the latch clicked its closure.

Sarah braced herself against the body of the four-wheel drive with her left hand and slowly took a step.

Walking a few feet to her side, Mark noted the slide of her right foot versus an actual step, but it was better mobility than she'd had at the MS walk. Her right arm, however, stayed stationary at her side. When she made her way around the vehicle, she stopped. There was about three feet between his bumper and the stair railing to her door.

Tentatively she took a step and wobbled. Her stubborn I-can-do-this attitude had gone on long enough. Mark wrapped her arm around him. "Lean in to me."

"I wish Karla were here." Sarah tried to look around Mark.

Mark's heart sank. He wanted her to wish for his help. Still unclear how she'd interpreted his earlier response as pity, he cleared his throat. "Sarah, I'm sorry I made you angry today. I only have your best interest at heart."

Sarah allowed him to lead her to her door.

"My backpack." She tried to turn, but his firm grasp didn't allow it.

"I placed it just inside the door."

She shook her head and reached for the doorknob. "You can let go of me now."

Mark released her physically, but emotionally he held on. "Sarah, I—"

"Enough." She held up her hand. "I thought you of all people would understand. After all, you told me that your mother led a full life with MS, just like I'm trying to do. Yet you are really like everyone else, full of pity for poor, sick Sarah." She twisted the knob and stepped through the threshold.

"Sarah, being overinvolved and living a full life are two different things." Mark took a step toward the door. Sarah's palm thumped into his chest.

"I'll be fine until Karla gets here. I thought you cared

for me, but now I realize you just took pity on me. Have a nice life. Good-bye, Mark."

Sarah hurled her words at him like a fast-pitched softball. Dazed and confused, Mark took a step back just before the door banged shut.

Chapter 11

The insistent rumble of Sarah's stomach forced her to hang up her office phone after being on hold with a carpet-warehouse employee while he checked the order mix-up for the new lessee's carpeting. Her boss wanted the issue resolved as soon as possible, but she'd have to call back later. She needed to take her medicine and eat lunch.

Sarah removed her Bible from her bag and headed back into the break room. She'd called in sick yesterday and gone to her MS doctor. The steroid shot she received at her appointment worked wonders for her leg. If she kept her stride slow, she managed her normal gait. Her arm was back to what she referred to as "MS normal." She sighed.

How had she been so wrong about Mark? Why did everyone else think they knew what was best for her? She was glad that Karla had insisted on Sarah's sleeping in and taking short naps for the remainder of the weekend, including Sunday, even though Sarah hated missing church. But the relaxing weekend and sick day on Monday had left her feeling refreshed and almost pain-free, not to mention clearheaded.

She stuck leftover Chinese in the microwave and uncapped her water bottle. Once her lunch was heated, she settled in at the table and opened her Bible. As leader of the summer Bible class, she'd chosen to study the book of Job, mostly for the same reason she wanted a quilt made from the Job's Tears pattern—a reminder that Job accepted his fate. He knew how to take the good with the bad, just like she accepted her MS diagnosis and all the changes that came with it.

"I missed you yesterday. What are you up to?" Ashley breezed past her to the refrigerator.

"Getting the lesson ready for my Wednesday morning Bible study." Sarah turned in her chair as Ashley grabbed an apple from the refrigerator and took a bite.

She walked over and stood behind Sarah. "You're studying Job. I always felt so sorry for him, the way the devil used him as a guinea pig. He endured all the bad stuff the devil inflicted him with, yet he still trusted God. That's the kind of faith we all need."

Sarah smiled, knowing she did have the faith of Job, trusting God, and He'd given her all these wonderful activities to take her mind off her disease.

"How'd the MS walk go?" Ashley planted herself on the folding chair opposite Sarah.

The smile faded from Sarah's face as the feelings of helpless humiliation rushed back to her. It wasn't bad enough that she fell in front of everyone, but then she gave in to her disappointment and weakness, thinking

Mark would understand. But instead of consolation she received pity.

"Sarah?" Ashley's brow wrinkled in confusion.

"Well…" Sarah sighed then turned in her chair and lifted her crop pants over her knee. "I fell about a block into the walk, so that's as far as I got."

"What? What happened? Did you trip?" Ashley leaned forward in her chair to study Sarah's injuries.

Ashley's concern-filled questions brought hot tears of relief to Sarah's eyes. If anyone would understand, she knew that it'd be Ashley. She actually cared about Sarah's well-being. "My MS symptoms tripped me up."

"I see." Ashley leaned back into her chair.

Her voice lost its previous concern. "Were you doing too much again? I know you put in long, stressful hours last week. I overheard your boss chewing you out about going over budget on the remodel project." She lifted her eyebrows.

Sarah shrugged. "It was just part of my job." It seemed that was really what the job was about, taking complaints from the renters, her boss, and now the construction crew. She missed the days that people were happy to see her bring a package through the door.

"I'm no doctor, but Sarah, I think you need to scale back. I think you should tell your boss that the construction project is just too much for you to handle."

"I can't do that!" Sarah's voice rose with each word. "I'll get fired." Why did everyone think she didn't need to earn a living?

"Well, there are many ways to make a living."

Had Ashley read her mind?

"Don't look at me like that." Ashley laughed. "Take me, for example. I'm a freelance writer and paralegal.

Surely you have other options than managing this building."

Young, hopeful, and optimistic—qualities in Ashley that Sarah admired. Yet they didn't really apply to a woman pushing forty who'd been diagnosed with MS. She'd taken the first job offered to her because she feared she'd have trouble getting hired at her age with an illness.

"Don't be such a skeptic." Ashley laughed harder. "I'm making it my goal to help find a better-suited job for you. One with way less stress. Let's see. Maybe a preschool teacher?"

Ashley continued to list obscure professions until Sarah finally laughed. "Okay, okay, if you find any of those job openings, I'll apply."

"Good." Ashley threw her apple core into the waste can beside the wall. "How's it going with Mark?"

Sarah's shoulders sagged.

"I see." Ashley touched Sarah's arm. "What happened?"

A flicker of anger still burned in Sarah at his reaction to her tears. However, it was no longer directed at Mark and his pity, but herself. Over the course of the weekend, she decided that, once again, she'd been a poor judge of a man's intentions.

"It seems I misread Mark's interest in me. He only feels pity for me, not love."

Ashley's eyes narrowed. "Are you sure?"

"As sure as I am that I have multiple sclerosis."

Jitters shook her insides as soon as Sarah pulled into the parking lot beside the quilt shop for her last class.

She'd tried to arrive as close to class time as possible. She didn't want to see Mark.

If only she could race through the store to the workroom, but she couldn't find her tote bag with the few completed Job's Tears quilt blocks and the remaining supplies to make a wall quilt. The last time she remembered seeing it was the day she helped Mark in the store.

So although she didn't want to see or talk to Mark, she might be forced to. Perhaps she'd get lucky and Terri would be working.

From her car, Sarah tried to peer into the plate-glass window to catch a glimpse of the salesperson on the floor. She was familiar enough with the routine of the store to know that someone would be at his or her dinner break.

Sarah fumbled around in her car, picking up trash and straightening floor mats for a few minutes until she saw Caroline arrive. That was when it occurred to her that she wouldn't be staying even if her tote was there.

She'd promised Caroline last week that she'd be caught up to the class with all the blocks completed and sewn into a top, ready to quilt. She didn't even have enough blocks completed to make a table runner. For a moment she considered leaving and cutting her losses. Instead she drew a deep breath and stepped out of her car.

Nervous apprehension knotted her stomach with each step closer to the door. She wanted to see Mark, yet she didn't. Over the weekend her feelings flip-flopped between apologizing to him for closing the door in his face or thanking him for the assistance he gave her, even though it came with a lecture. She'd been flabbergasted when Karla suggested she call him on Sunday evening to let him know that she was feeling better. In the end she decided that it could wait until tonight. And now she hoped to avoid him altogether.

The jangle of the bell seemed amplified as she braced for Mark's normal greeting to customers. However, it was a woman's voice who called, "Be right with you!"

Terri. Sarah's heart wrenched. Tears of disappointment threatened her eyes. She swiped at the dampness with her fingertips. What on earth was that all about? Yet she knew. She'd expected Mark.

Sarah waited by the cash register and watched Terri approach from the clearance section of the store.

"Hi, Sarah. Did you need something before class starts?" Terri eyed the clock above the door.

"I can't seem to find my tote bag with my class project. I remembered having it with me the day I helped Mark." Sarah's voice cracked as she said his name. She cleared her throat. "The day I helped out at the store."

"I know Mark really appreciated your help those two days. We get so many compliments on that patriotic display. I think your tote is in the back room, right where you left it."

As Sarah opened her mouth to tell Terri that she'd never made it as far as the back room, the store's front door opened. Sarah's heart betrayed her as it skipped a beat in hope that Mark would come through the door. The overwhelming disappointment threatened her eyes again as the two elderly ladies returned Terri's greeting.

"I can't believe six weeks have passed. Can you?" The friendlier of the two ladies looked at Sarah and motioned for her to join them walking back to the class.

"Um…no." Sarah guessed she should go back and see if her bag was on the table. She wondered if Caroline would allow her to sit and sew a block while the others learned to start quilting their project. If not, she'd make her apologies to Caroline and the class, and leave.

Sadly, Karla was three for three. Sarah's job wasn't right for her. The quilt class wasn't right for her. And Mark wasn't right for her. She wouldn't be in this situation if she hadn't been inflicted with MS. Self-pity began to weave its way through her thoughts.

Sarah allowed the elderly women to walk into the workroom first. Caroline instructed the other two classmates on how to pin the project together for quilting. Sarah's eyes rested on her tote on the table beside the sewing machine she used. The memory of Mark's demonstrating the machine tugged at her heart. A phantom feeling warmed her skin where his hand had cupped hers.

She might have told herself that she didn't want to see Mark tonight, but she did. She sighed as she picked up her tote, ready to make apologies to everyone in the room. The heaviness surprised her, and then she noted the girth of the bag. Slowly she sat down and pulled the contents from the bag.

"Ouch." She flinched as her finger met a straight pin holding the back fabric and batting to the quilt top.

"Wow, Sarah, you were busy this week. Hold your project up for the class to see." Caroline clapped her hands together, as if her voice didn't hold enough surprise.

Confused, Sarah shook her head. "I don't think this is my project." Yet the fabric did match the color scheme she'd chosen for her Job's Tears quilt. Carefully, she unfolded the lumpy square.

"It's beautiful," the young girl exclaimed.

"Yes, it is." Caroline lifted a corner and ran her hand over it then looked up at Sarah with a twinkle in her eye. "I was so surprised when Mark called and asked me to bring a hand-quilting hoop for you tonight since he'd just sold the last one he had in inventory."

"Puts mine to shame." One of the elderly ladies shook her head.

"I…" Sarah looked around the room at the class. "I didn't make this quilt. There must be some mistake." She laid the quilt on the table and smoothed her fingers over it.

Caroline came back with a large wooden hoop. "Isn't this your block?" Caroline pointed to a block that's pattern was misshapen. "And this one."

"Yes, but the rest…" Sarah's voice faded. She looked at Caroline, who wore a mischievous grin. "Did you finish my quilt top for me?"

Caroline's laughed echoed around the room. "No, I didn't." She winked at Sarah. "Mark must have little elves that come into the quilt store at night, like in the shoemaker story."

Sarah wrinkled her brow in confusion as she took the offered hoop.

Caroline stood close and whispered. "Maybe I shouldn't have said 'little elf.' Maybe I should have said 'a handsome elf.' " When Sarah looked her way, Caroline smiled wide and put her index finger over her lips to shush the conversation.

"I'll get you started with the running stitch." Caroline pushed the needle in and out of the fabric several times. "I'd follow the seam line if I were you." Caroline ran her finger along where she thought Sarah should hand quilt. "You won't get your project hand quilted tonight, but I'll make arrangements to meet you here and show you how to finish the raw edges when you have your project quilted." Caroline started to walk away then turned. "There's no expiration on that offer, so don't feel rushed."

Sarah hardly heard the instructions. Did Caroline mean that Mark had finished the quilt? Before trying it herself, Sarah studied the simple running stitch Caroline had started on the quilt held tight in the hoop frame. Though the layers were thick, Sarah managed the up-and-down motion of the stitch. She rested her arm on the table, which helped ease her control of her right arm.

Mark couldn't have finished her quilt. Maybe Terri or her daughter had. Sarah would definitely ask Caroline after class.

As Sarah found a rhythm to the stitching, something Ashley said about Job popped into her thoughts. *"He endured all the bad stuff the devil inflicted him with."*

Job did nothing to bring on his misery.

But I have been. Sarah gasped. Had she been so intent on taking the good with the bad that she'd been overdoing?

Mark had told her that he couldn't keep up with her schedule, and he didn't even have MS. He'd also told her that overdoing wasn't living a full life.

Sarah stopped stitching and traced the pattern with her fingers. She'd likened herself to Job all these months, and in reality, she was nothing like Job. She took the first job she'd been offered because it was temperature controlled. She volunteered for every church committee she could so her thoughts wouldn't wander to her future. She'd negotiated that lease with absolutely no knowledge of how wrong things could go with remodel projects. She'd filled her days with activities because she hadn't really trusted God to get her through the bad times.

Yet He *was* getting her through the bad times. What would she have done without Mark and Karla this weekend?

Sarah fought the urge to bury her face, pins and all, into the downy quilt and cry. Even after she'd locked him out of her life by closing the door in his face on Saturday, Mark finished her quilt because he knew how badly she'd wanted a wall hanging. Or was it because he felt the same way about her that she did about him?

She'd been so wrong. Mark wasn't like the other man she'd thought she'd loved. How could she have even compared Mark to her past mistake? Could he forgive her? Would he forgive her?

Sarah purposely parked her compact at the far end of the strip mall's parking lot. The pounding of her heart echoed in her ears. She drew a deep breath, thankful for the cool Canadian air that moved the jet stream. The unseasonable heat wave laced with high humidity blew out of the area. Between that and the weekend rest, her MS symptoms were again under control.

Last night in the quiet of her room, she'd had a long conversation with God. Through tears of regret on how she handled her disease and the people in her life, she'd promised to trust Him, just like Job.

As she walked down the sidewalk, Sarah smoothed her hands across her yellow crop pants and fidgeted with the ruffles down the front of her blouse. When she approached Mark's store she peeked into the plate-glass window in hopes of catching a glimpse of who was working. Mark stood at the cutting counter, no doubt cutting fat quarters. He wore her favorite shirt, the dark green polo that deepened the emerald hue of his eyes.

Sarah stopped by the window where the large orange-and-black Help Wanted sign hung. With her heart pounding faster she stepped through the door and angled herself out of Mark's range of vision.

The jangle of the door buzzer prompted Mark's pat response. "Be with you in a minute."

Running her fingers under the tape, Sarah loosened the sign from the window. She held it behind her back and walked toward the cutting counter, her flip-flops slapping against the tile floor then against her heels.

When Mark looked up, surprise etched his features. He laid the scissors on the counter, crossed his arms over his chest, and rocked back on his heels. "Sarah." He glanced at the clock on the wall. "What are you doing here this time of day?"

Sarah wanted to run around the counter, throw her arms around him, stare into his beautiful eyes, and beg his forgiveness. Instead she decided to let the cutting table be a buffer in case Mark didn't share her feelings. "I took a personal day. I needed a break."

Mark started to move his lips then pursed them together. He didn't need to speak. His eyes conveyed the message. Finally.

Fighting hard not to break his eye contact, Sarah cleared her throat. "I came to apologize and to thank you."

Mark dropped his arms, and a slight sparkle shone in his eyes. "Okay."

"I'm sorry that I jumped to a false conclusion on Saturday. Can you ever forgive me?" The fear of rejection sheened her eyes with moisture, but she saw a slight nod of Mark's head.

"I'd like to apply for this position." Sarah pushed the Help Wanted sign across the cutting counter toward Mark.

"Are you kidding me?" Anger flashed through Mark's features as he dropped his arms. With a swoop of his hand he pushed the sign to the end of the counter.

He strode around the counter, stopping in front of Sarah. Her only line of vision was his thick chest that heaved with his sharp intake of breath. His exaggerated sigh rained hot breath on the top of her head.

She willed her amusement out of her eyes as she lifted them to meet his face.

"You already do too much. You don't need to add a part-time job into the mix." Mark placed his hands on her upper arms just under her shoulders and squeezed. "You have to realize your limitations with MS. Your physical condition on Saturday tore my heart out."

Emotion deepened the green highlights of Mark's eyes. "Sadly, I believe most of your misery was self-inflicted. You might not care about your well-being, but the people who love you do."

Sarah's legs weakened. Not a result of her MS symptoms but from the rapid thump of her heart. Had Mark just said he loved her? She lifted her hands to Mark's biceps and leaned into his strength to steady her shaky limbs.

With her small movement, Mark shifted his arms and pulled her into a tight hug. She rested her head against his chest the same way she had on Saturday. Joy, mixed with regret, weaved in and out of her heart as if it were quilting it together. How had she mistaken his concern for pity?

The sea-kissed scent of Mark's cologne calmed the tides of her emotions enough for her to pull slightly away. She needed to look into his beautiful eyes. She needed to tell him that she loved him.

She drew a deep breath and searched his face then tilted her chin until it was a hairbreadth away from his. Once their eyes met, the joy-filled tightness in her chest expanded, and her need to tell Mark she loved him overtook all of her other emotions.

"I love you, too," she managed to whisper just before Mark's tender kiss stopped her from voicing all the other things she'd planned to tell him.

Sarah jumped at the first tinkle of the door buzzer, putting an abrupt end to Mark's sweet kiss. He squeezed her as he whispered in her ear, "To be continued."

Heat rushed to Sarah's cheeks as she watched Mark approach his customer. She could tell by the shake of his head that whatever the person searched for, Mark didn't stock.

The lady thanked Mark as she walked out the door. A giddy smile lit his face when he returned to Sarah. "Perhaps we should go to the back room." He walked over to her with outstretched arms.

Sarah grasped his hands with hers. "First, while I'm thinking straight, I need to tell you a few things."

Mark interlocked their fingers and lifted his brows.

"On Saturday, I thought you were pitying me, but then I realized that was my emotion. I'd been pitying myself since the doctor diagnosed my multiple sclerosis. Can you ever forgive me?"

"Yes I forgive you, but you have to stop overdoing.

I'm not hiring you part-time." Mark's features and tone took on a serious edge, but he never released her hands.

"I'm going to stop overdoing. You and my mom and Karla were right. I've been doing more than I did before my diagnosis. I was trying to prove to myself that I could still lead a normal life. I wanted the good to outweigh the bad, but what I was mistaking for good was actually bad for me. So I decided to make some changes."

Sarah laughed out loud at the skeptical look on Mark's face.

Mark raised his brows. "And those changes would be?"

"First, I'm never enrolling in a quilting class again when I can't sew, no matter how cute the quilt store owner is."

The sparkle in Mark's eyes deepened those gorgeous green flecks. He showed his thanks by lifting her hand to his lips and brushing a kiss to the top before rubbing it gently across his cheek. His clean-shaven skin soft and silky.

"Second, I'm going to limit my extracurricular activities to church or MS committees."

She earned another kiss to her other hand. "Excellent choices. Anything else?"

Sarah drew a deep breath. "I plan to quit my job."

The evident surprise on Mark's features tickled Sarah. She tried to suppress a giggle but failed. "After I worked here in the quilt store those two days, I realized how much I didn't care for my current job. It's too solitary and demanding, so I thought I might try working part-time. That is, if you'd consider a woman with absolutely no sewing skills as an applicant for your job."

Mark's expression went blank. "Sarah."

Her heart dipped. She wasn't really qualified to be a paid employee in the store although she hoped Mark would let her try. "It's okay, you can think about it." She understood if he wanted someone with sewing abilities. After all, it was a quilt store.

"Oh…and I need to thank you for finishing my Job's Tears project." Sarah didn't try to fight the impish grin.

A sheepish look settled on Mark's face, and he shrugged.

Sarah laughed. "I thought you didn't know how to sew."

Mark studied the toe of his shoe before raising his eyes to hers. "Just enough to demonstrate the machines I sell."

Sarah cocked an eyebrow. "I have it on firm authority—"

"Caroline." Mark huffed. "Okay, I know how to sew and quilt."

"Why didn't you tell me?" Sarah stepped closer to Mark.

"It's not a very masculine quality."

Sarah marveled at the stocky man before her that made her feel so secure and loved and couldn't believe he worried about being masculine. "That is something you don't have to worry about. So what do you sew?"

With some hesitation, Mark looked around the store. "All the projects on display in the store and some of the quilt tops."

"Well, thank you again for getting my quilt ready to finish. It's beautiful. I'm trying to spend an hour a day on the quilting. So far it's working out well with my MS."

"I knew it meant a lot to you. And you mean a lot to me. That's why I want you to take care of yourself. I've waited a long time to find you. Now about that job." Mark pulled her close and kissed her forehead. A thrill shivered through her as he trailed kisses down her nose. Certain this meant the job was hers, with a slight jut of her chin she positioned her lips to receive his, but he pulled away and smiled at her.

"I don't want you for an employee." Mark's features remained merry, but that didn't stop her gasp.

She opened her mouth but no words came out.

Gently Mark pushed her gaping mouth closed and held one finger over it to shush her in case her words decided to gurgle out. Was he still upset with her? He couldn't be, not with that mysterious grin.

"I think I need a partner rather than an employee."

Sarah's eyes widened. She hadn't planned on investing in a business. She started to protest when Mark's finger again applied light pressure to her lips. "Let me finish." He shook his head, and the sparkle in his eyes grew brighter. "You'd make a great partner, but the problem is this has always been a family-owned business."

A muffled squeak of delight passed through Sarah's lips. Her heart raced. Was he insinuating what she thought?

Mark removed his finger and dropped to one knee. "What do you say, Sarah? Would you like to be my partner for the rest of your life? Will you marry me?"

Sarah sat down on Mark's bent leg. "Yes." She didn't wait for him to initiate the kiss. She cupped his face in her hands. As their lips met, her heart expanded with love, and she finally understood what Job had meant.

God had counterbalanced the one bad thing in her life, her disease, with Mark and all the people who loved her.

* * * * *